LETTERS
I'LL
NEVER
SEND

LETTERS I'LL NEVER SEND

A NOVEL

NICOLE ZELNIKER

atmosphere press

To Beatriz, Elizabeth, Leah, and Rachel,
who gave me the confidence
to tell Sadie's story.

TABLE OF CONTENTS

"Dying is an art, like everything else. I do it exceptionally well. I do it so it feels like hell."
—Sylvia Plath, *Lady Lazarus*

"With all your faults, I love you."
—Billy Porter, *Kinky Boots*

<u>COMING HOME</u>

So much of what happened in the psych hospital is blurry, like I'm looking at it through glasses with a prescription that isn't my own. The moments that stand out the sharpest are with my wife Zora, who came at least once a week every week for eight months. A few times she brought our daughter Marina, but it was hard to get our daughter to come inside, and more than once she wouldn't. I can't blame her. If it were up to me, I wouldn't have been there, either.

I do remember getting out. Zora came and hugged me like she would never see me again. She pulled away and put her hands on my face. I bent forward until our foreheads touched. "We're going home," she said. I nodded and took her hand.

After eight months, I finally checked my texts and emails and messages. Several people had heard I'd gone off the deep end, apparently, and wanted to wish me well.

My brother had sent me stupid gifs and funny dog videos with text always along the lines of, "Hey Sis, you're locked up, but this made me think of you" or "Something to make you smile when you get out of the nuthouse." Most of them did. One of my closest friends from high school had messaged me long paragraphs about how much I meant to her and how she hoped I was all right. I hadn't seen her since my son died.

My daughter Marina is the clearest memory I have from the days immediately after the hospital. She had just turned six the month before, in March, and as soon as Zora and I got home she ran to me with the widest smile, her arms outstretched. "Mommy!"

"Hi, Bunny," I said, stroking her hair as we embraced. Zora smiled behind her, almost identical in their joy, even though Marina was adopted. People frequently think Marina is her biological child when they're out alone. People thought the same thing of me and my mom when I was growing up, Kate being a tan white person and me being a light-skinned Latina. My brother being Korean actually simplified the issue. People just assumed we were a package deal.

"I'm so happy you're home," Marina squeaked, squeezing me tighter. I'm sure I was reabsorbing my surroundings—the yellow walls, the pictures of our families by the TV, the coffee table Zora had taken from the sidewalk outside—but most of me was focused on the girl in my arms.

"I'm happy to be here," I said, and looked up at Zora. She smiled at me again, but smaller, sadder. She knew I only half-meant it.

"Give me the gossip," I said. "What's been going on for

the last eight months?"

"Uh, well, your mother called. She wants to see Marina."

"Oh. What did you tell her?" We were sitting on the couch in oversized sweatpants and T-shirts under a quilt Zora's mother had made for our wedding. Before, we might have gotten wine. The doctors had said it was best if I didn't drink for a while, though. Alcohol being a depressant and all that. Plus, the Prozac.

"I said that would be your decision."

"Thanks."

"She won't hurt her, Sadie. I'm okay with whatever you want to do."

She squeezed my hand, and I nodded. Zora's parents had abandoned Chicago for New York after I'd been admitted, so it's not like our daughter was growing up without grandparents. I just didn't know if Kate was the kind of grandparent I wanted for her. "Anything else?"

Zora picked at the skin around her nails, a bad habit she did when she was nervous, or just lost in thought. I couldn't tell exactly which it was. Finally, she said, "Kim's cancer is back."

I sat up straighter. "Is she okay?" Kim Salazar and her husband Terry Hamilton were two of our closest friends, and two of the only people who visited the psych hospital in the months I was there. Terry had been a researcher at the hospital where Zora worked as a doctor, until he got an offer at a hospital in New Jersey. Still, they'd driven out to Brooklyn at least once a month while I was in treatment.

"She started chemo last month," Zora said. "I'm sure she'd love to see you."

Had she looked any different last month? "Yeah, of

course." I took a shaky breath. I had never seen Kim sick like that, but I'd known she'd had cancer as a kid and then again in her 20s. And I knew that it could come back. "Anything less shitty?" I asked.

"Well, Marina loves school," she said. "Leslie Rogers and Katrina Jackson are both in her class."

"Why do all her friends seem to have first names for last names?" I asked.

Zora laughed. "Only you would notice that."

"Mama?" We turned. Marina stood in the doorway.

"You ok, Bunny?" Zora said.

"I'm not sleepy."

Zora went to get up and I put a hand on her knee. "I got her." Zora nodded and sat down again.

Marina eyed me warily as I bent down to her level. "Did you try counting sheep?"

"Counting. . . sheep?"

"Yeah. You picture them going over a fence and count—"

She peered around me. "Mama, do you count sheep?"

"Sometimes."

"Can you come help me do it?"

Zora looked over at me. I looked away. "Yeah, sure," she said. I kept my head turned as she led Marina down the hall back to bed. When I heard the door close, I folded up the quilt and went into my and Zora's room.

***

I didn't know what to expect from Rosa. I've seen at least a dozen therapists total since the age of nine (including the one in the psych hospital), and I wasn't keen to repeat any of those experiences. Zora got a name from Terry, though, whose brother's friend had seen Rosa and gave Terry rave reviews, so I figured I'd give it a shot. She looked accessible, at the very least. Her glasses were round and black, Harry Potter style. She wore a bubblegum pink sweater and jeans, and as far as I could tell no or minimal makeup. This made me feel better, since I'd barely had time to brush my hair before heading over to the appointment.

First sessions are a bit like first dates, in a way. You're both sizing each other up, figuring out if this is a relationship you'd like to continue.

Rosa's office reminded me a bit of Zora's at the hospital where she worked, a hospital different from the one where I'd been a patient. The desks were both a dark wood and both women had photos of their families on the walls. In Zora's office, she kept a photo of the three of us just above her computer, so she could look at it whenever she wants. About two months after that photo was taken, I became pregnant with Asher. The following year, I'd attempted suicide.

I settled on the pale blue couch across from Rosa's chair. "It's good to meet you, Sadie," she said.

My teenage self might have said something like "Yeah, my mom is paying you," or "Is it really?" The latter briefly flashed through my mind on my way to my mouth. I squashed them while they were still in my throat and instead said, "It's good to meet you too."

"So, I read a little bit of your file from your doctors at Cedar Hill," she said, fiddling with the silver necklace she wore. "But could you tell me in your own words about your experiences?"

This was new to me. No therapist before had asked me to relay my own experiences. They usually just believed Kate.

"Okay," I said. I realized my arms were crossed and put them at my sides. That felt awkward, so I moved them to my lap. "I tried to kill myself about two months after my son was born and, you know, died." I took a breath. "It was an in vitro pregnancy. The doctors said I had post-partum."

"That's the pragmatic retelling," Rosa said. "What do you remember feeling?"

"Oh, uh, I don't really know," I said. "It's all kind of blurry when I think about it. I know I went to the beach and, you know, wanted to die, but I can't remember how it, uh, how it felt."

"That's okay," Rosa said. "I understand you're a writer?"

"Yes," I said. I'd published two novels, one in my early 20s and one almost three years ago. The first one had been about a young woman meeting her birth parents, the second about young girl-turned-teen learning to live with her mom's suicide. "I mean, I don't make enough money to live off of it or anything. I taught creative writing at Cedar High before the hospital."

"That's fine," Rosa said. "I just meant that maybe it would help to try and write these things down. Turn them into something more accessible to you."

"That—" I considered it. Nothing else had worked so far. "I could try that." I might as well.

***

Kim being Kim, when I asked to come see her, she invited me to chemo. "It'll be fun," she said. "We can talk about you being a nutcase and you can watch me vomit into a bucket." She was already hooked up to the drugs when I came in, but she reached for me anyway. "There's our favorite psycho."

"Kim, please," Terry said, even though he knew I didn't mind. Kim had been in and out of therapy since she was first diagnosed with leukemia as a kid. Instead of shutting down and pretending it wasn't happening like I used to do, she joked about it. I liked that, honestly. It made me feel less alone, more normal.

Terry got up and gave me a hug. "How are you?"

"I'm okay," I said. "I saw Rosa this week."

"Do you like her?" Terry asked, sitting again.

I sat on Kim's other side. Kim was taller than me and had significantly more muscle than I did—perks of teaching karate I guess—but she seemed so small in the chair, like it was going to swallow her whole. She reached over and squeezed my hand. The place on the arm where the IV snaked into a vein was decorated with a large blue and purple bruise, a symptom of cancer.

"I like her a lot," I said. "She's having me write down some of what happened. I guess to make it more real to me."

Kim snorted and let go of my hand. "Sounds like she's giving you homework."

I ignored her. "We talked about writing letters," I said. "Like, not letters to send, but letters to different people in my life."

"Homework," Kim muttered.

"I mean, I always liked being a student," I said.

Kim laughed. "I'm surrounded by nerds," she said.

"You love us, though," I said.

"I suppose," she said, smirking at Terry.

"Excuse me, so we've already talked about me being a nutcase," I said. "When do you start puking into a bucket?"

"Ah, you missed that fun," Kim said. She leaned back and closed her eyes, looking more like she belonged in a tanning bed than a hospital chair. "Don't worry. Odds are I'll get sick plenty more times before this whole recurring nightmare ends."

"Delightful," I said. "How are you doing, Terry?"

"He's got some big medical conference in a few weeks," Kim said. She waved her hand in his direction. "Tell her about that."

"I'm presenting my research," he said. "It's really not that big of a deal." He smiled when he said it, though, the liar.

"Congratulations," I said, smiling too. "Where's the conference?"

He glanced over at Kim, who was watching him now out of the corner of her eye. "It's in Tokyo. . ."

"He's worried if he leaves, I'll die," Kim said.

Terry frowned. "That's not—"

"It is," she said.

"Babe."

"Sadie will take care of me," Kim said. "Right, Sade?"

"Duh."

"Well, see, there you go," Kim said. "All set." She leaned back again and closed her eyes, sending herself somewhere far away.

THE FIRST LETTER:
THE GHOST OF ME

Dear Krishna,

Our first date was perfect. You asked me to ice cream and we split two scoops: banana and caramel. You ate slow, so I ended up eating most of it. You insisted on paying, and I didn't say no. It's a habit from childhood, when my mother, brother, and I were a hair away from homeless. I learned to swallow my pride and let other people pay for me when they ask, even when they expect me to contradict them or offer to pay at least half. It is something I've come to anticipate.

You didn't seem to expect a counter offer, though, and we sat there talking until the man behind the counter started to shoot us dirty looks. He wanted to close up shop. We went to a bookstore instead because I had said how much I liked them.

I didn't intend to ghost you. In fact, after that first date I thought we might be together for a while, just casually. You planned to go to law school the next year, away from New York, but neither of us was looking for something serious at the time. With each date, though, I felt more dread leaving my apartment. Anxiety weighed down on my lungs and made each breath its own effort. We had gone on three dates when you texted me to ask if I wanted to see *The Book of Eli* in theaters. I didn't, and I didn't particularly want to see anything else with you, either. That wasn't your fault. I never wrote you back, and you never checked in.

It hurts to be ghosted, and I know that. That hasn't stopped me from doing it several times, when I'm overwhelmed, depressed, or anxious. Just because I know it's wrong doesn't stop me from doing it. It just means I feel bad about it later. I bring a whole new meaning to the cliché, "It's not you. It's me."

Several years before you, I ghosted another girl, then a pre-law student who was vegetarian, like me. We had every interest in common. We liked the same pizza place in Bed Stuy and fangirled over the same books and movies. The biggest difference between us was that she had grown up religious in a way that I, in my reformed Jew-ish household had not. She had never read *Harry Potter* because her parents feared witches. Most of the '80s and '90s pop music I knew by heart she had only learned about as a college student. Her childhood instead had been supplemented with Christian rock.

If anything, this made her more open, more excited to learn about new things. She told me about how, in college, each of her friends would teach her about their different interests, until she became an amalgamation of the people she knew best. Much of what were now her likes and dislikes matched mine as perfectly as they would have if I had designed the date myself.

And yet, I found my mind wandering when she spoke. There was nothing between us, no connection. When she kissed me in a subway station in lower Manhattan, I had my eyes open the whole time. I perseverated for days over whether or not to give her a second chance. When she texted me to ask what I was doing that weekend, I didn't answer.

I tried to ghost another girl, someone I'd met weeks before and whom I'd not been compatible with either, but for different reasons. From the first, she was insecure, seeking validation in the way she compared herself to me and awkwardly referencing when she would meet my family. When I didn't respond to her asking for a second date, she sent me a message.

"Can you at least tell me what I did wrong?"

I cringed at my Nokia—then the latest—and asked my friend to help me draft a response back. She did, and I wrote something along the lines of, "I'm sorry. I was wrong not to text you. I didn't think we had chemistry, but I should have told you that earlier. Wishing you the best with everything."

I thought I had done all right, until she sent another text that said, "It really hurt my feelings."

We went back and forth for a while, me apologizing again and again and her telling me that she was going to "die alone" and that "you really can't tell chemistry from one date" and that "you shouldn't ghost people," which I thought would have been obvious, even if I did it anyway.

Near the end, she said, "I guess that's it, then. You can go ahead and block me now." Which, honestly, didn't make me any more inclined to give her a second chance.

Colbie was the last person I dated before I met you, you being the last person before I got together with Zora. We went on three dates, the same number of dates you and I went on together. We too got ice cream together, in DUMBO, and sat down by the water before going back to her apartment. We talked about shitty first dates in Brooklyn and how we were both adopted. She showed me the view of the Manhattan skyline she had paid an obscene amount of money for. She kissed me against the New York City backdrop, and we went back to her studio.

On our second date, we watched *The Blind Side* in theaters. It wasn't nearly gay enough for us, so we went back to her apartment after and watched *Imagine Me and You* instead, the one where Piper Perabo fakes an atrocious British accent and ends up with Lena Headey. We had sex that night for the first time, and I fell asleep in her arms. I left at some ungodly hour the next morning, Colbie's eyes still shut.

That third date, we got dinner at a vegan diner in Williamsburg and saw Foster the People at a crowded bar. She didn't invite me back that night. She had a going away party for a colleague she was going to make a spectacularly late entrance to. The next morning, I texted her that I'd had a great time. She texted me back that she really liked me, but didn't have time to date, really. Did I want to be friends?

Colbie didn't ghost me, so I can't say I know how you feel. And I really don't know that you liked me the way I liked Colbie. I berated myself for getting too attached after three dates and told her that I was sad, but I hoped the best for her. With Colbie, I felt a flutter in my chest that I hadn't felt since high school and that I wouldn't feel again until Zora. Maybe it was silly, since we hadn't known each other for very long. That's what I told myself then anyway.

I don't really know why I'm writing to you. I haven't spoken to you in years. I wouldn't know how to get this letter to you, even if I wanted to send it. I guess I'm writing you this letter because I know that you deserve an apology. You were a sort-of rebound after Colbie, even though I suppose you can't really rebound from someone you were never dating. You were good and you cared and you wanted us to be happy together, just spend time. I'm sorry I didn't want the same.

I suppose part of me also feels the need to apologize for dating you before I was truly ready. I know I can't stop the anxiety and the depression and the desperation I felt when I thought of spending time with you. It's something I've struggled with for a long time, but I've come to accept that it's sometimes out of my hands. But I shouldn't have said yes to a date before I had these things under control at least a little bit.

It's been years, and you've moved on, but I do want to say that I wish you the best, Krishna, in a different way than the others. I wish you the best because you're a good person who happened to be fucked over by someone in a bad place. You deserve to be happy. I hope you are.

All the best,
Sadie

FAMILY TIES

"You don't want to see it?" I'd brought the letter just in case, printed.

"Not unless you want me to," Rosa said. "I'd be happy to look at it."

I shrugged. In truth, I'd been a lot more honest than I thought I'd be in my letter, and I didn't know if I was ready to share that with Rosa in our second session, even if she already knew the whole mental health history. "Maybe another time."

"That's fine," she said. "Anything on your mind today?"

"Umm. . . My cousin messaged me," I said.

"How are you related to this cousin?" Rosa asked.

"They're my father's sister's kid," I said. "I haven't spoken to them in a long time. Apparently. . . my father is trying to get in touch with me."

"And he asked this cousin to contact you."

"I have him blocked," I said. "I haven't spoken to him since I was fifteen."

"How do you feel about this?" Rosa asked.

I laughed. "That's such a therapist question."

"Well, good thing that's my job, then," she said, smiling.

"I don't really know. Avery—that's my cousin—Avery and I used to be super close when we were kids. But I guess I don't really know them anymore. We exchange 'happy birthdays' and stuff like that, sometimes."

"Are you thinking about responding?"

I shook my head. "That's a definite no," I said.

"Have you talked to anyone else about this?"

"Just Zora and my brother know they reached out. My mom and I have. . . a complicated relationship."

"Oh?"

"We actually hadn't spoken for, well, two years before the psych hospital. Two years and a few months. We had a really big fight."

"Do you mind telling me what it was about?"

"Marina, mostly. My daughter. We adopted her about three years ago now, and Kate just wasn't very supportive."

"I assume she did something other than not be very supportive if you didn't talk to her for over two years."

I laughed. "She asked if. . . it was too late to return her. To return Marina. Because Kate thought I wouldn't make a good mom."

"That's harsh."

"Yeah." I shrugged. "She called Aaron crying when she found out I'd been taken back to the psych hospital. Since, you know, I was admitted once before, as a teenager. He told me and I told him he could bring her."

"So, things have been a little tense."

I nodded. "That's one way to put it."

"Have you seen her since you left?"

"No," I said. "She keeps asking me to."

"But you're not ready." It wasn't a question.

"She's a lot. I guess I'm still trying to get in a good headspace for me. I don't really think Kate makes for good headspace."

Rosa smiled. "That's really good, actually. You can't let her needs above your own."

I couldn't help it. I smiled back.

***

"Uncle Aaron is here!" Marina yelled, running into the kitchen seconds after the doorbell rang.

"You can open the door," Zora said, and Marina sprinted off to greet my brother. We could hear her giggling from where we stood, and a moment later Aaron appeared in the doorway.

"Everyone's favorite uncle brought dessert," he said, placing a store-bought cake on the counter.

"Thanks, Uncle Aaron," Zora teased. I went in for a hug.

"You look good, Sis," he said.

"Why thank you. Maybe you should try eight months in the psych hospital."

Aaron nodded, as if truly considering it. "I do think it would do wonders for my skin," he said.

"Marina, help me set the table," Zora said.

"Let me look at this cake." I grabbed Aaron's arm and

steered him toward the dessert he'd bought from the bakery down the street. Not that I minded setting the table or anything, but I still remembered the look Zora gave me when I'd offered to do it last week, after I'd picked up the knives.

I love Aaron, but I swear, I thought he was never going to leave. Marina didn't seem to want him to, and he was perfectly happy chatting on and on about our stupid childhood antics. The time I cut his hair and Kate walked in on her daughter with scissors in her hand standing over her nearly-bald son. The time we were playing hide-and-go-seek and I hid in a laundry chute.

When I told Marina it was almost time for bed, she gave me an odd look and continued talking with my brother like I hadn't spoken. Finally, after she'd had practically fallen asleep at the table, Zora carried her off to bed, and Aaron grinned at me, food-sleepy, from across the table. "I love how much Zora loves you."

"I love that too," I said. Was I blushing? Just a bit, probably. I didn't blush easy. Unfair, because I didn't even have wine to blame it on. But thinking of Zora did that to me.

"One day, I'll have a Zora," he said. "Well, not a Zora, exactly, because your Zora is a lesbian."

"Well, I wish you the best of luck in your search for a non-lesbian Zora," I deadpanned. "What about Lily?" Lily owned the bar that Aaron and his musician friends frequently played at in Manhattan. Last I'd heard, she was getting a divorce.

"Nothing is happening between me and Lily."

"Yeah, sure." I'd never met Lily, but I knew from Aaron that she had pink hair and a moon tattoo on her neck. She was Chinese, and her parents were immigrants. She was a twin. Basically, I knew way too much about this woman for my brother to not like her a little bit.

Aaron got quiet, contemplative. He looked down at his plate and squashed a leftover cake crumb with his fork. "I went on a couple dates with a woman recently," he said. "It went really well, until I told her I, you know, wasn't born a guy." I waited, and Aaron continued, "I know the right person won't care and all that, yada yada, but it still kind of sucked, you know?"

"I'm sorry," I said. "Really."

He shrugged. "It bothers me. And then I try to remember that you still love me and Marina pretty much worships the ground I walk on."

"Not 'pretty much,'" I said. "She absolutely worships the ground you walk on."

Aaron grinned. "Exactly. And even Mom tries, sometimes."

"Mmhmm." It had been years since Aaron had come out—he had just turned 12—and Kate still sometimes spoke about him with the wrong pronouns.

"I'm really glad you're doing okay," he said. "I mean, I know it still hurts, and you're not, you know, perfect, but I can tell you're doing better. It's a little scary when you're not."

"I know," I said. "I'm sorry."

"No." Aaron shook his head. "No, no, no. You were sick, Sade. You don't get to be sorry."

"Yeah, yeah."

Zora walked back into the room. "I'll put these away," she said, gesturing to the dishes. "You did last night."

"I can still help," I said. "I'm not the one working a full-time job."

She waved her hand. "Aren't you supposed to be writing?"

"Yes, ma'am," I said, giving her a small, sardonic salute.

"I guess that's my cue to leave." Aaron stood. Finally. "I'll be by soon?" He hugged us both and left. As soon as he was out the door, Zora turned to me.

"Now you," she said. "Write."

Nothing. I stared at the screen, tapped gently on the keys, and sighed. Should I just start? *I felt like I wanted to kill myself.*

Backspace, backspace, backspace. Fuck that.

I went to the ocean wanting to die. . .

Ugh. No. Not that either. Finally, I typed, *The moss between your toes is smoother than you thought it would be, and somewhat sticky. It creates a barrier between your soft skin and the rough rocks. Though you suppose it doesn't matter if you cut your foot on a particularly jagged edge. Tonight, you plan to die, and soon none of it will matter at all.*

Yes. That felt right.

You've come to the ocean for your final resting place. You've been coming here for years. First, with your mom and brother and later with Zora and Marina. On a more practical note, you don't want your wife or daughter to find you bleeding out in the bathtub or hanging by a rope in the closet, especially your daughter.

The water settles briefly against your calves before it rises up again, hovering around your knees. It is colder than expected in September and a welcome reprieve from the repressive air. Perhaps the result of climate change somehow? You don't plan on ever finding out.

You lift your arms above your head and take another several steps, until you're no longer on the rocks and now stepping on soft sand. In the pocket of your denim shorts, your phone must be short-circuiting, the first of the two of you to drown. Another step and you lower your hands into the water. The ocean licks at a paper cut on the side of your left hand. You hiss and nearly pull it back when you remember that all of you will have to be submerged eventually.

A wave comes on the next step just as you stumble off a sandbar. It soaks the bottom half of your white blouse and the tips of your dark hair. You take a final step, then dive.

The sounds of the city are never so obvious as when they disappear so suddenly. The rattle of the Q train on the elevated subway tracks. The shouts of cross-faded teens and their top 50 pop music further down the beach. And the smells—of hot dog stands and car exhaust. Just gone. The absence of all your senses weighs down on you with the water until you break the surface, gasping for air.

It is a shame you can't do it here, but even you who never cared for biology knows that your body would rebel. Your lungs would scream for oxygen and your traitor legs would kick up. First, you must exhaust yourself.

You don't remember the first time you went to the beach. Your mother must have brought you when you were just an infant, and you know there are pictures of you and Aaron from when you must have been two or three, Aaron hardly older than a fetus. It has always just existed for you. When you tried yoga that one time in college, you used the *ocean as your happy place.*

For as long as you can, you use the breast stroke. It will get you the furthest from shore and possibly unwelcome salvation. It feels like too soon and still not soon enough when your lungs begin to beg for a break. They don't know that they're about to be pushed to their absolute limits.

Once you can't swim anymore you slip your head under the water. The shoreline vanishes behind you and the lone boat on the horizon disappears ahead, replaced by murky darkness. You take a deep breath of sea. Your lungs spasm and your heart thuds in your chest, as through it's working to free itself from its rib cage prison. Your legs don't betray you, but your arms do. They scramble for the surface at first until you force them to your sides.

The painful thudding in your chest slows and your lungs accept their share of sea water. You hope you don't bloat too much before someone finds you, for your family's sake. Your limbs grow heavy and your ears begin to pop as you sink, but they sound far away. They feel far away, too. Is that possible?

The last thing you are aware of, the last sense that is lost to you, is your vision. The water is dark around you, blotting out the stars and the sky, but bright white lights of your own form as you shut your eyes. Your vision clouds and the small circles appear. They are dandelion-like, little puffs exploding behind your eyelids. They are fireworks, a celebration.

I shut my laptop as Zora walked into the bedroom. "How's it going?"

"I mean, I wrote," I said, twisting around in my desk chair. "That's good, I guess."

"I'm proud of you, Sadie," she said, putting her hand on my shoulder.

I stood and pressed my forehead to hers. "Thank you." I placed a gentle kiss on her mouth.

She opened hers. "Sade—"

"Let me love you?" I asked. I felt her nod and kissed her again, deeper this time, and she kissed me back. We fumbled like teenagers for each other's clothes and stumbled onto the bed. For the first time in perhaps a year, I made love to my wife. When we were done, and when we lay on our sides of the bed tangled up in each other, I wiped the tears off her cheeks.

"I love you," she whispered. "I was so scared."

"I won't leave," I said, holding her tighter. "I won't leave."

GUILTY AS CHARGED

The first thing you are aware of is the taste of seawater and vomit burning the inside of your mouth. Then, the voices whispering overhead. Not whispering—it just sounds that way as you come back to yourself. Soon, you realize they are speaking, then shouting. You recognize the movement then of being in a car. No, an ambulance. Under the shouting voices you hear a siren blaring. You feel the IVs snaking their way along your arms and hear the humming of machines you've come to associate with pregnancy and birth. This is your last thought before you black out.

You resurface in the hospital and panic when, for a moment, you think you are about to hear the news again, that your son has died, and there is nothing you can do to save him. Everything looks the same: Zora to your right, sleeping fitfully in a metal chair. The tubes that bring fluids to your arms. How did they rescue you? You will later learn you washed up on shore, that one of those drugged-up *teens risked arrest to call 911.*

When Zora opens her eyes and sees you are awake, nei-ther of you says anything. There is nothing to say. Well, you could say you're sorry. But your wife is perceptive, and is already anticipating the lie. Instead, you communi-cate with a look. You tell her you love her.

I know. I love you too.

That you never wanted to hurt her.

I know that.

What now?

Finally, you do speak. Where is Marina? Your voice is distorted and scratches at the sides of your throat like claws.

"She's with Aaron," Zora says. "My parents are coming up to, to help. . ."

To help? That must be the first time it clicks. That you are not going home. Your eyes fill with tears, and you turn away from Zora. She puts a hand on your arm. You bury your head in the flimsy hospital pillow beneath your head and will sleep to come.

I shut the laptop when I saw Talia walk in across the cafe. We'd been best friends in high school and recon-nected after she moved back to New York after grad school. She was beautiful in a beige top and the chai neck-lace I'd gotten her for the big eighteen a million years ago. She wore her light brown hair in a ponytail, Ariana Grande style. She saw me at a table in the back and nearly ran to me. I stood as she got closer, and she enveloped me in her arms. "I'm so glad to see you," she said. "How are you?"

"I mean, you know, been better." I shrugged. "Been worse."

"Oh, yeah. For sure," she said, grinning. "But really. I'm glad you're okay."

"I would have liked to see you." I hadn't meant for the words to come out, but now that they had, I kept going. "You know, if you had come to the hospital. Just once."

Talia hesitated. "I really should have. It was really hard to think of you. Like that. It's not an excuse." She stood. "I'm going to get coffee," she said. "Want anything?"

I held up my latte and shook my head. Talia left to get her coffee. She came back after a minute and said, "So, have you heard the news about Madison?"

"Who?"

"Madison Carver? She took bio with us, like, freshman year of high school."

"Uh, no?" She went into the details about Madison getting addicted to opiates after a car accident and having a meltdown and going to rehab. She's heard it from an old friend who saw it on Facebook.

"Isn't that awful?" she asked, sipping her coffee.

My hands tightened around my own cup. "Is she okay now?"

Talia shrugged. "That's all I know," she said. We didn't talk about the psych hospital again.

***

"Can I ask, why Krishna?"

I blinked. "Sorry?" It was my fourth appointment with Rosa, and she still hadn't read my letter, but we had talked about it, and she got the gist.

"I don't mean that in a bad way. I just meant you could choose to write to anyone. Why her?"

"Oh. I guess she's someone I haven't spoken to in a while. It's easy when the relationship is, well, complete, you know?" I'd thought a lot about who to write the first letter to. Not Zora or Aaron, since I would have let them read anything I wrote anyway. Not Kate, not yet. That would come later. Eventually, I settled on someone in between. Not someone I would ever send the letter to, but someone who I didn't have so much emotional baggage with either.

"Still, I'm sure there are a lot of people you don't talk to anymore," Rosa said. "You only knew her for three dates a long time ago."

"I feel guilty, I guess. Not just with her, but she's the one that I think deserved getting ghosted the least."

"Even if it was wrong to never message her back, you know that you couldn't have helped the anxiety, right?"

"I mean, yeah."

"I know you *know*," Rosa said. "But you still feel like it's your fault, don't you?"

I hesitated. "I— Yeah, maybe. I guess I feel guilty. . . for a lot."

"What do you mean?"

"My friends and family, mostly. My brother Aaron came by last week and he mentioned, you know, that it's scary to see me in, uh, I guess in a bad way. Which, of course it is. I can't be upset that he feels that way."

"Why does that make you feel guilty?"

"I don't want him to be in pain because of me. Because of something I should be able to control." I hesitated. "That came out wrong. I meant because of something I want to be able to control."

Rosa frowned and shifted in her seat. "Sadie, your

mom came to see you in the hospital, right?"

"A bunch of times," I said.

"How did she react?"

"She cried," I said. "She said she couldn't stand to see me in pain. She asked me to get better."

"Like it was something you could control."

"Mmhmm." I laughed. "Damn, yeah. I guess that makes me feel guilty."

"Have you ever told her this?"

"Honestly, I'm kind of realizing this right now," I said.

"That's therapy for you."

"It's all that and— My friend Kim, she has cancer. She's gone through this three times already and I guess I feel weird that. . . that I wanted to end my life. When she's fighting so hard for hers."

"I'm sorry," Rosa said. "If you don't mind me asking, what kind of cancer?"

"Leukemia."

"That's blood, right?"

"And bone marrow."

"So you wouldn't tell your friend that she isn't sick because it's only in her blood and bone marrow, right?"

"That doesn't make sense."

"So why are you less sick because your disease is in your brain?"

I actually laughed out loud. "I guess this is why I'm paying you, huh?"

"Actually, your insurance is pretty good," Rosa joked, smiling. "You're not paying me much."

***

How do you deal with her? You ask Aaron this one day after you've cut Kate out like a cyst. You try not to think about her often, but sometimes, you can't help it. This is one of those times. He takes a moment, thinks about it. Eventually, he says, "She's my mom."

She doesn't respect us.

"I know."

So. . .

Aaron shrugs. "I can't not have her around. Do you know what I mean?" *You say that you don't, and he says,* "I'm not like you. You're independent. Strong. I've never been okay with being alone." *You have never considered yourself strong before. You suppose not everyone could have made the decision you did, but what is the alternative? You cannot keep Kate in your life, not like this. You might explode.*

I'm not strong, you say, and Aaron shakes his head. "I think you're too strong," *Aaron says.* "That's why it's so hard when you have to fight against your own brain."

***

"I'm glad it's helping," Terry said. I'd driven out to Jersey for the day, needing a break from my computer screen. Zora had dropped Marina off on her way into work, and I would be back in time to pick her up. I owed them both that much.

"Really, thank you for referring me." We sat in the living room, me on the chair and him on the matching couch. Their house was small—one floor—with exposed brick and hardwood floors and all that other stuff that couples were supposed to look for when they bought a home.

"Anytime," he said. "How's Marina doing?"

"She seems okay." I shrugged. "She's. . . adjusting still, I think." Terry waited for me to continue, so I said, "I mean, it sucks to go through this, but the part I honestly hate about this the most is that I'm dragging her through it too."

"I've thought a lot about that," Terry said. He glanced backwards, toward the bedroom, where Kim was asleep. She'd had chemo the day before. He turned back to me and said, "We both wanted to have kids, when we got together."

"Why didn't you?" Terry sighed, and I said, "You don't have to answer that if you don't want to."

"No, I brought it up for a reason. Kim couldn't get pregnant after, you know, all the drugs. And none of the adoption agencies would give us a kid because—"

"—because Kim had been sick." I looked up at Terry. "I had no idea."

He shrugged. "Why would you? I just think about it now and, would this all be so much worse if we had a kid?"

"Honestly?" I thought about it for a moment. Would it be better for Marina if we hadn't adopted her at all? Finally, I told Terry, "I can't say."

We both looked up when the door to Kim and Terry's room opened. Kim came down the hallway, stretching. Her eyes were just a little bit bloodshot. "You missed chemo," she said.

"I'll have to come next time," I said. "Can't have you having such a good time without me."

"Of course." She sat down next to Terry on their couch.

"'m tired."

"Your body is going through a lot," he said, putting his arm around her. She leaned into him and put her head on his shoulder.

She turned to look at me. "Did you meet Rodney last time?" I shook my head and she said, "He's an old guy who does chemo at the same time as me. I'll introduce you."

"Can't wait."

"Can I get you something?" Terry asked her.

"Uh, you want to make tea?"

"Sounds good. Food?"

Kim made a face. "Nah."

"Okay." He kissed her forehead and got up, and Kim pulled her sweatshirt tighter around herself. She sat back against the cushions. "How are you doing?"

"I'm okay."

"Don't pull that bullshit with me. How are you?"

She always knew. "You were right. It was kind of homework. But I think it's the good kind? It's really hard, but cathartic too."

"Good. I'm glad you're getting something out of nerd therapy."

"You could be less of a jerk, you know."

Kim shrugged. "I could," she said. "I won't, but I could."

"You can't change her," Terry said, coming back into the room with three mugs. He set them on the table and leaned over Kim.

She reached up to meet his lips with hers. "Hmm. You wouldn't want to," she said. Three small bruises dotted the side of her neck.

THE SECOND LETTER: BONDED

Dear Avery,

I considered writing this letter to my father, but couldn't think of how to begin. So I have chosen you instead, you whom I will use as a proxy for him, the closest I can get to my childhood without having to delve into it too deeply.

You and I are bonded by family, or so I'm told. When I tell people I don't have any cousins, they ask if my parents have any siblings, and I say that my mother is an only child, even though she isn't, but that's complicated too. When they ask about my father, I say nothing. That tiny, infinitesimal space between nothing and just a hint of something, that is where you and I are related.

We used to be close, as kids. You and me and Aaron and Johanna saw each other at least once a year, every

Christmas in Colorado. This was where Aaron and I learned how to skate, on the pond that froze over in your backyard. I vaguely remember slipping on skis down the bunny slope by your house, and your overjoyed reaction when I made it to the bottom unscathed. That was the first and last time I'd ever been on a ski slope.

Did you know that I never learned how to ride a bike? My father—your uncle—started to teach me once, when I was eight or nine. After he left, we never tried again, and Kate became too busy with divorce proceedings and parenting two small children by herself. I saw you rarely after that. The last time I saw you in person, in fact, I was thirteen, and you had come to New York with your mother and my aunt to my Bat Mitzvah. It had already been four years, and the cousin who used to be my best friend was now a stranger, looking over at me half-heartedly with blank eyes and wondering why they were there.

I almost saw you once in New York. We were twenty-four or twenty-five, and you had come with your then-boyfriend to Manhattan. I messaged you and asked if you wanted to get together downtown. You said yes. Not two hours before we were supposed to meet, you texted and canceled. I don't remember what your excuse was. Just that I was uncomfortably relieved.

I do think about you, sometimes. When your birthday comes up on Facebook or when I see you post about life events—your wedding, various graduations—on Instagram. Kate lived in fear for a while that we would be in touch. Not because she didn't want us to be. I don't know what you remember of her, but she always liked you and Johanna. She just feared that I or Aaron would tell you what our father was really like behind closed doors, and that you would tell your mother and your mother would tell him. She was afraid of what he might do in court if his family knew we had revealed his secrets, of what he might say or do to his children.

In this letter that I'll never send, I can paint you a picture. In a movie, I could cast my father as the hero, super-manning me up into the air with strength amplified by childhood adoration. In our house, he would take me and Aaron into his arms and throw us to the high ceilings. He was Mr. Incredible, the strongest man on the planet. The safest I felt then was in the air, inches above my father's waiting hands. In my child brain, I flew. Even after he moved out, some of my favorite days were Central Park picnics with him and his friend Jen on almost-summer days. Once, he took us on an adventure to a chocolate fair, a dream for Aaron, the chocolate king. In winter, we would sit in his apartment and watch *The Princess Bride* every week. He would keep the Christmas tree up far past its time if I demanded it. It was as Aaron and I wished.

I memorized the streets by his apartment so that if I ever got lost, I could find my way to a then-semblance of home. I remember the cracks in the sidewalk and the men in orange hardhats working on construction of some sort or another. They weren't interesting. They were just landmarks.

Or else, I could cast my father as the villain, someone to overcome. As a child I used to beg Kate to stay home from whatever errands she had to do that day in case my Clark Kent father became a monster instead. Sometimes it didn't matter if she was there or not. One night, he pinned me down because I wouldn't look at him when he spoke to me. I was embarrassed that I had been crying because my third-grade math homework hadn't made sense. After that, I still wouldn't look at him for fear of the fury on his face. Kate stood there and screamed.

When he came to pick me and Aaron up for visits he would sometimes come inside the house. In a memory, he and Kate argued in the hallway while Aaron watched a Disney sequel in the den. I don't hear them in this memory. Just see their lips moving, him grabbing her and shaking. I leave with him. When I come home, the cops are still on our front porch. My father started picking us up at the local Dunkin' Donuts after that, and Kate waited in the car.

The most apt role for my father would be that of the stranger, someone like you. Slowly, and then all at once, I missed our weekly meeting at Dunkin' and spent my Saturdays at home. I don't know when we stopped being father and daughter, but it was before Aaron's Bar Mitzvah. Johanna came to that one, as though you alternated being envoys for this branch of the family you would have perhaps preferred to prune. In a photo we took together, he put his arm around me. "C'mon, Sade," he whispered before the camera clicked, "pretend like you know me," because I didn't really. This was the last time I saw him.

I don't know when I stopped knowing where his street was, either. He moved away to New Jersey after a while, and then to Virginia. I don't know where he is now, and I wouldn't want to. I came across the street, once, and still knew it, though the construction had been completed and the men in hard hats replaced by throngs of impatient New Yorkers. More recently, I realized I wouldn't know that street if I walked past it again. Now, I don't know that I would recognize his face if I ever passed him on a busy Manhattan street. He would be just another pedestrian to me, someone outside of my life.

Maybe I would have told you if we had stayed close, but I really don't know if I would have. You had your own relationship, although sometimes I feared that he would hurt you or Johanna. I don't even know now if you would believe me, we have been apart for so long. Maybe I would just be some crazy woman to you, with beliefs of a twisted childhood that aren't true. I suppose I will never know, and I have to be okay with that.

Wishing you well,

Sadie

PRESSURE

My job at the library was an absolute joke. I was making minimum wage and working three mornings a week, but Rosa and Zora both said that it was a start. Aaron came by after work most days on his lunch break and took me out.

"Any new lady prospects on the horizon?" I asked.

"When you say it like that, it sounds creepy," he said.

"Whatever." I took a bite of my burger. Aaron had convinced me to try Beyond beef, apparently all the rage now. It actually wasn't bad.

"I think I'm taking a break from the whole dating thing," he said. "Maybe we'll try again come fall."

"What are you, Kate all of a sudden? You get summers off now?"

"Ha, ha." Aaron bit into a fry, and waved it my direction. "It's so funny I forgot to laugh."

"Chew with your mouth closed," I said.

He swallowed. "Have you seen Talia lately?" he asked.

My cheeks flushed. Aaron was the only person besides Zora who knew that my supposed best friend of over two decades hadn't come to see me in eight months. "I— a few weeks ago."

"How'd that go."

I shrugged. "She apologized for not coming to see me. And then we talked about other things."

Aaron swallowed another fry. "If it were me, I'd be mad."

"Good thing it's not you, then."

"You know what I mean," Aaron said. "Honestly, I love Talia, but she can be really selfish."

"She said it was hard."

"I promise you, Sade, however hard it was on all of us, it was hardest on you." He took another bite of his burger and I shrugged. I'd been through this before, when I was fourteen and locked up on an adolescent psych unit for a week. Then, Aaron had said similar things about Kate. She would cry and tell me how devastated she was and Aaron, then twelve, would pull me aside. "It's not about her," he would say. "Don't let her get to you."

"I know," I said, taking a fry. "It doesn't make it not hard for the rest of you, though."

***

God only knows how I let Kim talk me into going to a boxing gym, but I did, and she was thrilled. "You'll love it," she'd said in the car. I'd picked her up on the way to her favorite place, which was really anywhere she could beat someone up.

39

"Sure."

"It's good for depression," she said. "Releases endorphins and all that."

"You're not supposed to be working out."

She rolled her eyes. "You don't know that." We stopped at a red light and I shot her a look. She shrugged. "I mean, I can work out a little bit."

"Yeah, like, taking a walk. Not hitting me."

She laughed. "Scared, Goldman?"

"I mean, kind of." Kim had been doing martial arts for forever. I wrote books.

"You know, that's fair." She shrugged, as though it was completely normal for friends to be scared of each other.

"You know I don't have—"

"I know. I brought you gloves and wraps and shit."

"You really want me to go get pulverized," I said.

Kim laughed. "It's fun! I promise."

"Fun for you."

"I mean, yeah. I think fun for me is fun."

"Harder!" I punched the pad on Kim's hand harder and stepped back.

Kim sighed and lowered her hand. "What now?"

"I'm just not good at this," I said.

"Look, Sade, you're being a pain."

"Thanks."

"You're not good at it because you're not trying." She raised her hand again. "We're going to stay until you get in a couple good punches, so keep at it."

I rolled my eyes, got back into position, and punched. "That was good," I said.

"Don't stop to analyze every punch. Jeez."

I looked up at Kim and froze. "You're bleeding."

Kim removed the pad on her hand and reached up to touch her face, just under her nose. She groaned when she saw the blood on the tips of her fingers. "Damn." She took quick strides back to the locker room, and I followed her. She leaned over the sink in the bathroom toward the back and held a paper towel to her face.

Her eyes met mine in the foggy locker room mirror. "Time out?"

"Are you okay?"

"Cancer thing," she said. "I got a bad one at work right before I left and scared the shit out of some little kids."

"Bet their parents loved that."

"They mostly forgot by the time their parents got there."

A group of women coming into the bathroom froze when they saw Kim. They seemed to hesitate, unsure if they should help. Finally, one of the women in a pink sports bra said, "Kim? Are you okay?"

"Yeah, fine."

Another one whispered something I couldn't hear, and they left. As soon as they were gone, Kim said, "The epitome of white suburbia. I know people everywhere." She chucked the towel in the trash can and took another one, holding it under her nose. "They know about my cancer, I think. They know that something's wrong, at least. They're just majorly uncomfortable." The blood seeped through the towel as she spoke.

"They seem. . . Yeah, 'uncomfortable' is a good word for it."

"You know, I hate saying 'my cancer' like it's something I own. I just don't know how else to describe it. 'The cancer,' maybe? 'That thing that's going to kill me. . .'" She paused, blew her nose, and replaced the towel. "Nose bleeds are one of the symptoms. I was tired too, before I realized it was back. Run down. But it was winter, and I work with kids, so I thought I was just regular-person sick. Or maybe I hoped."

"What made you realize?"

"Combination nose bleeds and bruises." She held out one of her arms to me, dotted with various yellow and green and blue splotches. "I don't bruise easy. Unless there's cancer in my blood."

"How did you tell Terry?" I asked.

"He didn't want to believe it," she said, examining the damage on the paper towel. "Not that he didn't believe me. But he was just so hopeful." She shrugged and tossed the towel in the trash can. "I told him when he got home from work and showed him the bruises and everything. It. . . wasn't easy."

I sighed and stood. "Well, if beating me up will make you feel better, I guess I have an obligation to let you."

Kim laughed. "I guess so," she said. She wiped the rest of the blood off her face and washed her hands. "Let's go again." She flicked the leftover water at the sink, stepped toward me, and tightened the too-lose wraps on my hands.

I studied her face. Pale, eyes unfocused. "Maybe next time, chief."

***

Everything is numb. You have no real concept of your body in the immediate aftermath of Asher's death except that it is there, heavy, an extra weight to drag around. Zora keeps Marina busy with friends so you can sleep. Aaron takes her to the Central Park Zoo one day, to the Museum of Natural History the next. You know they both worry.

Guilt worms its way into your mind. They wouldn't feel like this if you weren't around. It isn't fair that Zora has to take care of you like this when she also lost her son. You start to form a plan in your mind, a plan that would mean the people you love most wouldn't have to worry about you at all.

Kim and Terry come by. Terry keeps his arm around you and Kim talks to you in a low voice about how you'll get through this, that there is another side. This is the closest you come to feeling like yourself again, like there is a way forward.

Close is not enough. Kim leaves, and the thoughts come back to fill the void. You begin to think about where you'd like to die almost constantly now. What you want your last conversations with your wife to be like. In the week before, Zora tells you that you seem to be doing better. You are happier, you think. You have something to look forward to now. A different way out. You ask her a few nights before, Has she ever wished she had a different life?

Zora lifts her head. "What do you mean?"

You shrug. You had been drifting off to sleep when the thought came out of nowhere, striking you like lightning. You ask her if she'd rather be married to someone without depression.

"I don't want you gone if—"

That's not what you're asking.

Zora reaches out for you in the dark. She takes your hand and your fingers tangle together, dancing in the faint shadows from the moonlight. "No. I never want to be with *someone else."*

But it would be easier—

"But it wouldn't be you."

You squeeze her hand. You say, Okay. You let Zora trail off into dreams, even though you don't believe her. Eventually, you let your dreams take you too. They are filled with images of your son, but they don't bother you anymore. You will be together soon enough.

***

The only reason Kate hadn't come to see me yet was because I kept making excuses. "I'm busy that weekend" or "Oh, I have lunch plans that day" or "Zora's busy, so I have to watch Marina." Finally, six weeks after I'd been released from the psych hospital, I ran out of excuses.

"Do you want me to stay with you?" Zora had asked. She had put the TV on mute when I told her.

"No, I'll be fine. Aaron offered the same thing, actually."

"Hmm. If you change your mind. . ."

"I can handle Kate," I said, sitting next to Zora on the couch. "I did grow up with her, you know."

"I mean, I suppose you turned out okay," she said, grinning. I rolled my eyes, laughing, and turned the volume back up on the TV. When as Kate showed up at our door that Monday, though, I almost wished I'd taken Zora up on her offer.

Kate was already near tears, her hug overwhelming. "My baby." She held me at arm's length. "You look too skinny."

"Thanks, it's the trauma."

"Not funny." Kate folded her arms across her chest. "Are you ready to go?"

I held up my keys. "Let's get out of here." I locked the door behind me and followed Kate to her car. She lived up in Westchester now, with easy access to a train that would take her into Manhattan, but she still insisted on driving everywhere. That should thrill Marina, at the very least. She loved it when we came to get her from school in the car, or at least she had in preschool. Maybe she wouldn't anymore.

Kate struggled with the parking meter for a bit before we went into Charlie's, a small French café in lower Manhattan. Kate wasn't the burger place type. "I want to take you out somewhere nice," she said.

"How do you think I function when you're not here?"

Kate sighed. "Well, I am here now, so we're going to eat nice." As though I meant I only ate boxed mac and cheese and beans from a can when she wasn't there, or didn't eat at all. Honestly, she probably thought that.

***

"I saw my mom this week," I said. "For the first time since I went into the hospital."

"How was it?" Rosa asked.

"It— it was."

Rosa laughed. "And that means?"

"We have a complicated relationship," I said.

"You know, I'd actually gathered that."

I felt the corners of my mouth twitching. "Aren't therapists supposed to be nonjudgmental and all that?"

"Hey, I'm not judging," Rosa said. "I'm just being

snarky. There's a difference."

"Uh-huh. I mean, we just went out to eat. And she went on and on about how much she'd been through and how I couldn't see her earlier and it just made her so worried, blah, blah, blah." I shrugged. "I sound ungrateful."

"Why do you think that?"

"She, I mean, she so clearly cares. Aaron and I are the most important things in her life, and I know that. It's just a little overwhelming sometimes."

"You're allowed to feel that way."

"Yeah."

"Have you told her this?"

"I have. She just thinks I'm pushing her away, usually. And that's not what I'm trying to do, but also it kind of is? Well, not push her away but make her a little less. . . intense?"

"Why does it matter that she's so intense?"

"It just feels. . . I guess it makes me feel anxious. Like when she's telling me all about how I look too skinny and she can see my sadness in my eyes and all that it makes me feel that way. Like I'm not eating enough and that maybe I am still in that bad place. And I want to be immune to that, well, suggestion. It's just hard because she's my mom. And when she says I worry her she makes it sound like I have the power to make it better. I want to do that, so badly. And then I realize I can't and honestly, it just makes me feel shitty."

Rosa nodded. "I can see why that would be a lot, yes."

"She talked about Aaron for a little while. And how she's worried he might be lonely and she wishes he would see her more. I really—this is kind of the worst part—I don't always mind when she starts on all that. I defend him, of course, and I know he does the same for me, but I honestly like not always having to be the problem child. Which so isn't fair to him."

"That's what siblings are for, right? Take some of the pressure off every once in a while."

"I guess so. And I think he'd understand. I'm sure he feels the same way."

"Could you talk to him about that? Would it make you feel better to know that he knows?"

"I don't know. Maybe."

DUMB LUCK

The park by Kim and Terry's house wasn't big, but Kim liked to go there on good days and take laps around the lake in the middle. On the days I made it up to Jersey—every other week at this point—I went with her. On the days she wasn't in school, Marina went to the pool with a friend, or she went over to her grandparents' apartment. Or else she spent time with—

"—Shauna. Her birth mom."

"Oh yeah. I met her."

I frowned. "You met Shauna?"

"At Marina's last birthday party."

"Oh." Of course, I hadn't been there.

Kim seemed to realize what she said and changed the topic. "Where do they go?"

"She took Marina to a movie last time. Something Disney."

"Cute."

"Kate hates it," I said. "She feels like Marina will get too attached and. . . think Zora and I aren't her real moms. . ."

"Well, good thing she's not Kate's kid," Kim said. "For real, you're both awesome moms, and fuck what she thinks."

"I guess."

"You know I'm right." A pause and then, "Can we sit down?"

I looked over at Kim. Since the boxing gym she'd lost some weight, enough that I could see her collar bone where I couldn't have before. Her chest was heaving and sweat dotted her forehead. We'd walked maybe a mile, halfway around the lake. It wasn't warm.

"Yeah, of course." I followed her to a bench a little further down the path. She stumbled over and sat down. She took a deep breath.

"Thanks." She paused, inhaling deeply. "Sorry."

"You don't need to apologize," I said, but I knew how she felt. I'd done the same thing.

She turned away from me, looking out onto the lake. "I worry sometimes what's going to happen to my body, even if I beat this."

"When," I said.

Kim turned back to me. "What?"

"When you beat this."

She rolled her eyes. "Your optimism annoys me."

"Really. I don't know anyone as strong as you."

"You don't know a lot of people." She sighed. "You don't beat leukemia three times."

"I mean, have you ever tried?"

Kim laughed. "No. I guess I haven't."

"You just have to, like, Mr. Miyagi it or whatever you do."

"Mmhmm. Exactly that. You should really be the one teaching karate."

"I do my best," I said.

"Is that what you did in the psych hospital?" she asked, nudging me with her shoulder. "Just beat the crap out of your depression with your fists?"

"Oh, yeah. That's what they teach you in therapy."

Kim laughed again. "At least we can be sick together, I guess."

"It's different," I said. "You don't beat depression by being strong. You beat it by not being weak." It churned my stomach a bit, that confession, but I needed to say it. I wasn't like her. I wasn't a warrior.

"Where the fuck did you learn that?"

"What do you mean?"

"You're so dumb sometimes. You're fucking resilient."

"Kim—"

"That's the bad mental stuff talking. It's telling you you're not the right kind of sick just because you don't look sick or have tumors and shit in your body. I promise you, it's not that different. You need the same stuff to beat it. You know, dumb luck and some drugs." She stood up. "C'mon. I bet I can still beat you back."

I got up and followed her. "If you take off running and pass out, I swear I'm dumping your body in the lake and telling your husband you died of being a moron."

***

Roni is the first person to tell you that you'll never get well. She had developed depression as a preteen, like you, and your mom had recruited her to come talk to you on the temple steps outside the sanctuary, recently remodeled to accommodate wide windows and more sunlight. Since you are in New York, that really only works for the half of the year that daylight savings pushes everyone forward an hour.

You hadn't wanted Roni to know what was wrong with you. You hadn't wanted anyone to know. It was embarrassing to be sick, especially with something so many people told you that you could control. But she is here, and so you ask her when she stopped having those thoughts.

She smiles at you sadly, her lips thin. "Never," she says.

Learning you will be sick forever thrills the little disorder demon growing in your mind. Several therapists have talked to you about thinking of your disorders—OCD, depression, anxiety—as physical, and so you imagine them all as monsters lurking in the recesses of your physical brain. The permanence of their residence pleases them all.

You are fourteen, and you have forgotten what it feels like to be happy. You take the dull edge of the razor blades you recently started using and slice them into your skin, taking the worst out of the emotional pain and replacing it with something physical. You prefer it this way.

You are twenty and in college, and you suddenly can't breathe. What if you fail your bio class this semester? Is the girl you're sort-of seeing going to tell someone that you have scars on your thighs? Do your friends still want to hang out with you after you made that dumb joke in the cafeteria the other day? No one has ever described this to you as a panic attack, so you do not know what it is or why your lungs have forgotten how to take in air. In, then out, then in, then in—no, then out, then in.

***

Aaron hated New York. When he left to be a musician in Boston, he promised he would never come back, until he realized that if he wanted to be a musician, he would pretty much have to.

It seemed like he'd invited everyone he knew to this gig he was doing in Chelsea, an opening act for an only slightly-less unknown band. A few days before Talia texted me and asked if I was going. I said I was. She didn't text me back, so I didn't know if she was coming until I saw her at the bar with her boyfriend Mark. They'd started dating just before I got pregnant with Asher.

"Sadie!" She waved to me with one hand and held a scotch with the other. I took Zora's hand in mine and she squeezed. She led me to the bar.

"You remember Mark?" Talia gestured to the man beside her in khakis and a polo shirt looking wildly out of place.

"Hi." I think we'd met once.

"Mark, this is Sadie, and this is Sadie's wife, uh, Zora."

Zora flashed a smile, teeth bared. "It's great to see you, Talia."

"I didn't know you were coming," I said.

"Yes, you did. We talked about it," Talia said. She shrugged. "You must have forgotten."

"Must have," I said.

"Who else is coming?" Talia asked.

There were already some people in the audience I rec-ognized—Aaron's college friends, a woman with pink hair who I realized was Lily because of the moon tattoo on her neck—but no one from the high school we'd all gone to to-gether. "Some of Aaron's friends," I said. "I don't think an-yone you know."

"Oh. Well—"

"We'll be right back," I said, grasping Zora's wrist. We weaved through the crowd in the direction of the bath-room, in case Talia was watching.

"Why do you put up with her?"

I looked back at the bar. Talia was laughing at some-thing Polo Mark had said.

"She was my best friend for so long."

"Sometimes friends outgrow each other," Zora said. I glanced back over at Talia. I opened my mouth to defend her and Zora said, "Just pointing out that you were the one who wanted to escape her just now."

"But—"

Applause. Aaron had appeared on the stage with his electric guitar. He waved out at the crowd. He spotted me and waved. I smiled and waved back.

***

When you are fourteen years old, you are the first per-son Aaron comes out to, sitting cross legged on your bed in your grandparents' house. He takes a deep breath and says, "I think I'm a guy."

What do you mean?

"Like. . . I'm not. . . a girl." He ran his fingers through his hair. He had cut it short recently. "I've been reading

about Karen Kopriva. Do you know who that is?" You shake your head, and Aaron says, "She was a teacher who. . . She was a man for a long time, and then she realized she was a woman."

You're not making any sense.

"She was transgender. And I am too." He looks at you with a mix of hope and fear dancing in his eyes. You say, Okay.

"Okay?"

Okay.

"What do you mean 'okay'?"

I mean, I believe you.

Aaron's face splits into a wide grin. "Really?"

You do. Aaron is your best friend, the person to whom you tell everything. Both of you had held whispered confessionals in your blanket forts about your frustrations with Kate, about your feelings toward your father, about liking girls. You're still not entirely sure what transgender means, but if Aaron says that he is a boy, then you believe him.

"Mom is going to flip, though," he says. Just a few weeks ago, you had come out to Kate as a lesbian, and she had laughed. She had said, "Good one. That's funny."

You shrug. You tell Aaron that he won't be alone. You will be there with him.

***

After, Zora and I lay wrapped in only our sheets and each other. She pushed my hair out of my eyes. "Goddamn, girl."

I laughed. "Goddamn yourself."

She twisted my hair in her fingers. "What are you thinking about?" she asked.

"Do you remember your surgery?"

Zora frowned. "Surgery?"

"Your appendix. We'd just started dating, and we were supposed to go see a show or get dinner or something, but you got really sick and ended up in the hospital. You told me you were getting surgery. I mean, I guess I thought I might hear from you later, but you called me almost as soon as you got out. There was just moaning on the other end and I was freaking out until your sister picked up and said you were fine, just drugged."

Zora laughed. "Poor Leah dealt with me though that whole time." She put her hand on my cheek. "I don't remember calling you."

"You were super out of it," I said. "That was when I knew you loved me. We'd been on like three dates and you called me."

"I mean, I'm glad my high self knew to send you a sign." She frowned. "I don't even think *I* knew that I loved you yet."

"What can I say? High Zora knows what's up."

"You're such a dork."

"You married me." I leaned forward and kissed her, pressed our foreheads together. "When did you know that I loved you?"

"Uh. . ." She wrinkled her nose, thinking hard. "Kate's apartment."

I pulled back. "Excuse me?"

"It was the first time I met her. We were there for Thanksgiving and she had a couple friends over, and I only knew you and I think I'd met Aaron once."

"Oh, God, that was the one where we fought about. . . What were we fighting about?"

"I don't even remember," she said. "You left the living room before she could make a huge scene and I followed you down the hall. You let me hold you while you cried. You were just such a private person; I think I realized then how much you trusted me. Maybe even loved me."

"Glad my turmoil is a cherished memory of yours."

"Oh, hon," she said, playing with my hair again. "All my memories of you are cherished."

THE THIRD LETTER:
MIND GAMES

Dear Lucy,

Even though Kate had never been to therapy herself, she made sure Aaron and I went after the divorce. You were our introduction to mental health care, a short, white woman with cropped hair and glasses. You wore button-up shirts and khaki pants. Your office was plastered with pictures drawn by your patients, and I hated them. My least favorite hung directly behind where you sat during our meetings, a picture of you covered in purple spots. To me, the spots looked like bruises.

We played a lot of Uno while you tried to get me to talk about my deepest secrets and fears. Mostly, I just lost at Uno. You would think a therapist specializing in young children would have the decency to let them win every couple of games. I guess not.

After several sessions, you came to the house to investigate the scene of the crime. I listened from the doorway as you told Kate that our father had left her because Aaron and I had toys scattered everywhere. No man wanted to live in a messy home. You left a note on the answering machine a few days later apologizing, but I never saw you again.

You were my first therapist, but certainly not my last. My next therapist was Phoebe, who I was convinced was named after the character from *Friends*, even though the show would have come out years after she had been born. It made perfect sense to nine-year-old me. Phoebe was the one who diagnosed me with OCD and introduced me to cognitive behavioral therapy, the bane of my existence for several years after that. She had me stop washing my hands on a loop, which drove me crazy, even though my hands had become cracked and bloody from too much soap. She had me hold on to objects that touched the floor without washing my hands. I held them until I screamed, and then she had me keep going.

I saw so many doctors, honestly, I don't know who of them were licensed therapists and who weren't. I saw two possible psychiatrists shortly after you, when I was seeing Phoebe. I later learned that they were part of the team that were to decide custody of Aaron and myself. One of them put me on Prozac, the first time I took an antidepressant. The other thought Kate had Munchausen Syndrome by Proxy, meaning she was making me sick as part of her own psychological disorder. And while Kate has her problems, that was pushing it.

I'm not well. I don't think there will ever be a "well." But I am better. I don't wash my hands until they bleed.

Before I became pregnant with Asher, Zora and I went on a pizza date where I got two slices, before I knew how many she would get. As an adolescent, I had to be the person eating the least, always.

I spoke about you with my new therapist. Her name is Rosa, and when I told her about the you-visiting-my-home incident, her jaw dropped. I told her that you had left a message the day after Kate let you go, apologizing. I had told Kate we should give you another chance. Not because I wanted to, but because I felt bad for you, making a mistake. When Kate found me a new therapist instead, I was secretly relieved.

Kate sat in on many of my therapy sessions, especially as I got older. Mostly, those sessions became a place for her to vent about me, about my disordered brain, about my misbehavior. You once lectured me during one of these sessions, not long before the home visit, for being a burden on her. In another instance, when I was fourteen, Kate didn't sit in at all but spoke to whomever I was seeing then for the whole hour while I waited in the lobby. I don't know if the later therapists believed her because she's older, or because she's louder, or because she was paying for the sessions, but I don't think they ever once asked me for my version of the truth. At some point, I stopped giving it.

I'd never been a fan of therapy for me, until Rosa. Part of it is her—she gives tough love, but she's also supportive in a way I hadn't found before—but it's also because for the first time in my life, I'm seeing someone alone, and I can finally speak my truth. And that truth is: it is a relief not to share that crowded room with Kate's words.

Lucy, I hope you're doing well. Honestly, I hope that

you felt bad about our interactions for a while, but I also hope you moved on. You made a mistake, and it was a bad one. Even though I'm glad I never went back, I hope you were able to help someone else. I'd like to think that you learned something from our time together, even if it turned me off to therapists for years.

Please forgive me if I sound condescending. I'm not nine anymore.

From,

Sadie

BLOOD AND BONES

Aaron and I both trudged up to Westchester for Kate's birthday. She had her favorite Italian place across the street from her complex, which is where we ate most of our meals when we visited. Somehow, God only knows, we'd stumbled upon the topic of sex and gender, the surest way to confuse Kate.

Kate sighed. "I couldn't have had a single normal child?"

"What is normal, though, really?" I asked, sharing exasperated eye contact with Aaron.

"Just, a boy who likes girls or a girl who likes boys."

"I'm a boy who likes girls," Aaron said.

"You know what I mean."

"We do," I said. "And it's offensive."

Aaron frowned. "You like Zora though."

"I never said I didn't like Zora."

"What are you trying to say, Mom?" he asked.

"That she doesn't want us around," I teased, jabbing my fork in Kate's direction.

"I never said that!" she protested. "How could you even think that?" She sounded like she was about to cry.

"It was a joke," I said. Only partially, but she didn't need to know that.

"Oh. Ha, ha."

"I mean, I'd feel a little more love maybe if you got my pronouns right," Aaron said. I snorted into my pasta.

"You know, it isn't easy for me," Kate said. "I grew up in a different time."

"Yeah, we get it, we know," I said. "Have you ever considered that maybe Aaron needed your support more than you needed his?"

"You guys are always ganging up on me," she said. Aaron shrugged, and we left it at that. "How's therapy?" she asked me.

"It's good."

"What are you guys talking about?"

Bite. Chew. Swallow. "You know, I don't really want to talk about my private therapy sessions with you."

"Oh, okay." She rounded on Aaron instead. "Are you seeing anyone?"

"Not right now," he said. "Living that bachelor life." He pumped his fist in the air. "Yay, me." I rolled my eyes. Had the two of us been alone, I would have teased him about Lily, who I happened to see congratulate Aaron after his set the week before. Never in front of Kate though, who had probably never heard her name.

"I hope you find someone someday," Kate said with a sigh. This time, I couldn't make eye contact with Aaron. I was too worried I'd burst out laughing.

"How's Kim, anyway?" Aaron asked pointedly.

"Who's Kim?"

"She's okay," I said, ignoring Kate. "She told Zora the other day that she wants us to make sure Terry dates again once she's dead." I rolled my eyes. "Like we're just waiting for her to kick the bucket so we can play matchmaker for her husband."

"Who is this?"

"She reminded Zora that Terry is, in fact, bi, which means we can really set him up with anyone."

"I feel like everyone is bi these days," Kate said.

Aaron sighed. "Ma. Do you mind?"

"You brought it up."

Under the table, I found his knee with my hand and squeezed.

***

It turned out Kim's chemo friend Rodney was a sixty-four-year-old white guy with liver cancer. "I was never even an alcoholic," he told me.

"Bad luck," Kim said.

"You know, when your friend here started, I bet her she couldn't make it fifteen minutes without puking after they started the chemo. She made it fifteen minutes and one second just to spite me."

Kim shrugged. "I wanted to win."

"You're both ridiculous," Terry said, and Rodney chuckled.

"You gotta have some fun," he said.

"I had fun winning."

Terry sighed. "Anyway, Sadie, what are you doing next

week?"

Kim groaned. "Terry, please."

"Nothing. Why?"

"Next week is the conference in Japan. Would you mind just checking in with Kim? Make sure she's okay?"

"I promise not to die while you're halfway around the world," Kim said.

"Of course I will," I said. I turned to Kim. "And you have no say in the matter."

Rodney sighed. "You get a little bit of cancer and all of a sudden they treat you like a kid."

"For real," Kim said. Terry's eyes stayed on her face. He opened his mouth to say something, then didn't.

***

"Can I ask you something?" I nodded and Rosa continued, "You adopted Marina, and you said you were considering adopting again, but that you really wanted to give birth. Why was that so important for you?"

"Oh. . . I guess I haven't really thought about it."

"Think about it now. What made you want to give birth over adopting or having a surrogate?" Rosa leaned forward in her chair, inviting me to speak. Very therapist of her.

"We had adopted. . . I guess I just never thought of giving birth as a possibility for me and Zora. When it was one, I guess I realized I just wanted to do it."

"But why?" Rosa asked. "What made it a better possibility than adoption, for example?"

"It's not better," I said. "Honestly, I felt a little guilty. About not adopting, I mean. I feel like I'm always supposed to be grateful, as an adoptee, and not adopting just kind of felt like. . . not being grateful." Super eloquent, Sadie.

"You don't have to be grateful all the time, you know," Rosa said. "You don't have to live your life as the poster child for adoption."

"That's what Zora said. She told me if I wanted to give birth, then we would find a donor."

"But why was it something you wanted to do?" Rosa asked again.

"I guess it's still about adoption," I said. "I've never wanted to know my birth parents, really. I mean, I was curious about them, but I don't feel like I'm curious enough to want to find them. But it still felt like it would maybe be nice to have someone. . . related to me. By blood. I'm saying it out loud and now it sounds silly."

"It doesn't sound silly."

I had only seen Asher once, before they took him away. He was mere minutes old when he died, but I saw me in him. The shape of his eyes. The curve of his nose. I felt tears welling and looked away from Rosa. "I don't need blood to make a family," I said. "And Marina doesn't mean any less to me. I really don't know why I wanted to do this so badly."

"You don't have to know," Rosa said. "That's part of being human."

"I guess so."

"How did you tell Marina she was going to be an older sister?"

"Oh, we just told her. After we found out I was officially pregnant. She was so excited." I bit my lip. Paused. "She. . . She's been acting differently. Since I came home."

"How so?"

"She just doesn't listen to me. She double checks with Zora when I tell her to do something. She wants Zora with her all the time—" I paused. My voice had caught in my throat. I cleared it and blinked tears back. "I just hope this isn't. . . forever."

"She's getting used to things," Rosa said. "Sadie, can you look at me?" I did, and she said, "Marina is really young, so this is a big part of her life that she has to read-just to. But kids are also really flexible. And from every-thing I know about you, you're a good mom." I wanted to believe her, then. But she didn't really know. How could she?

Still, Rosa smiled at me. "She'll come back to you," she said.

***

You don't get visitors in the psych hospital during the week, and you happen to be admitted on a Monday. Most of that first week is a blur of activity. Seeing doctors and therapists and attending group events and experimenting with pills. Another two patients are admitted, and three leave. A young woman—perhaps in her twenties—with manic-depression tries to befriend you on one of her good days. You ignore her. You don't have good days yet.

On Saturday, Zora is the first visitor at the hospital. She holds you close, and you break down in tears. She spends most of the time reassuring you that Marina is okay—she is with Aaron—and that they aren't going to abandon you. It is your biggest fear. You have never dis-cussed that, but Zora knows.

Aaron comes the next day. The two of you talk about

the hospital and compare it to the one you stayed in when the two of you were kids. This one is nicer, you agree, but you tell him you liked the doctors you had at the other one better. He does not tell you yet that Kate wants to visit. That will come later.

Zora returns the next week, fulfilling her promise. She tells you that Marina started Kindergarten and shows you photographs of your daughter, smiling. In one, a candid, your daughter does not smile. You think you see a shadow pass over her face, one you've seen in the mirror before. You don't let on to Zora how much this hurts you.

Kim and Terry visit you the day after on that second weekend, and you tell them this because you can't keep it in. You are embarrassed when you start crying. What if they leave you too? Instead, they both come to you and hold you close. You cry holding both of their hands and leaning on Kim's shoulder. They hold you up.

***

"Mo-ooooms!"

Zora and I ran to Marina's room, where it looked like our apartment had been hit by a hurricane. Clothes lay strewn on the floor and drawers hung out of her dresser.

"What happened in here?" Zora asked.

Marina stepped forward in her karate uniform, the one from last year. She'd closed the top with her blue belt, but it still gaped open in the front. "My uniform doesn't fit."

"Oh. You couldn't have asked us to find it for you?"

Marina shrugged. I hid my face behind the door so she couldn't see me laughing.

"I need one that fits so I can do karate with Auntie

Kim."

Zora and I glanced at each other, any trace of suppressed laughter gone. We'd had Marina enrolled in Kim's class last summer on the weekends, but I didn't think either of us remembered how much she'd loved it until now.

"Bunny, I don't think Kim is going to teach karate this summer," Zora said.

Marina frowned. "Why not?"

I crouched down to Marina's level. "Remember how we said Kim was sick?"

"But that was a long time ago," Marina said. "Why isn't she better?"

I glanced up at Zora, and then back at my daughter. She didn't seem concerned. Just confused. "This isn't like when you get a cold," I said. "Kim has a longer sickness."

"Oh. Is she going to get better?"

I bit my lip. Zora put a hand on my shoulder and answered for me. "We hope so," she said.

Terry texted me later that night from Japan. 'Nothing alarming—just wanted to let you know Kim has a cough and a low-grade fever. She'll try to hide it from you.'

I sighed. 'Thanks for telling me.'

Honestly, it was a miracle Kim had let Terry know this at all. As if he read my mind, he wrote, 'She wouldn't have told me either. I only know because we FaceTimed.'

Zora walked into our room. "Our daughter is asleep at last." She sat next to me on the bed. "You ok?"

"Mmhmm." I put the phone down on the table next to me. "Is it—Is it weird that I'm so scared for Kim when. . . I wanted to die?"

Zora's mouth tightened around the edges. "I don't

think so," she said.

"I feel guilty."

She frowned. "About?"

"Kim doesn't want to die, and she still, you know, might. And soon." I took a breath and continued, "I just don't think that's fair."

"It wouldn't have been fair if you had died either," Zora said, taking my hand. "This isn't your fault."

"Yeah."

She kissed my cheek. "It'll be okay," she said, and in that moment, I wanted so badly to believe her.

COME BACK TO ME

It wasn't until I started hammering on the door with no answer that anxiety kicked in and I really thought Kim might be dead just inside. "Kim!"

The door opened and I stumbled forward, nearly knocking into her. "Oh."

Kim had her arms crossed, dressed in black sweatpants and a green tank top. She uncrossed her arms and held up her phone. "You called me ten times."

"Yeah, to make sure you were still alive."

"I was sleeping," she said, and opened the door wider to let me in. Her eyes were red-rimmed and glassy, as if instead of sleeping she'd been up on a three-day bender.

"It's noon." I stepped in and slid my shoes off in the hallway. "How are you feeling?"

"I'm alive," she said. "So you got what you came for."

I rolled my eyes. "You have soup in the fridge still?" Kim nodded and I said, "I'm heating it up for you."

Kim threw up her hands. "Fine." She sat on the couch in the living room while I went into the kitchen, really part of the same room, separated by a half-wall. Behind the kitchen-living room divider, I could hear Kim coughing, stifled, as though she was hoping to suffocate the sound. Kim wasn't usually an if-I-can't-see-it-it's-not-happening person, so I had to assume this was for my benefit.

"How's Terry enjoying Japan?"

"He likes it a lot," she said. "He's gotten to go to all these nerdy medical panels."

"Sounds great for him." I took the soup out of the microwave and brought it to Kim, who had thrown a thin yellow blanket over her shoulders. She reached forward when I put the bowl down, and I felt her forehead.

"What are you doing?"

"You have a fever," I said.

"A fever isn't what's going to kill me," she said, picking up the spoon.

"You're such a pain," I said, sitting next to her. Wasn't fever a cancer symptom? I'd looked it up a few weeks ago, but now I couldn't remember.

"Love you, too, Sadie." She picked up the remote and turned on an old sitcom rerun. "Don't you have things to do?"

"Perks of being psychotic," I said. "I don't have a full-time job."

Kim coughed behind her hand and said, "Happy for you."

"How's Kim?"

I glanced over at the couch. Kim had fallen asleep not ten minutes into a particularly bad rerun. I'd moved to the chair after I'd covered her more fully with the blanket. "I mean, she's sick," I said. "I think she's trying to hide how sick she is."

On the other end of the call, Zora sighed. "Sending her my love."

"I'll let her know," I said. "You'll be home for dinner?"

"Yeah. I'll ask my mom to pick up Marina from school, okay?"

"Sounds great. Love you."

"Love you." I hung up the phone, lost in my own thoughts for a minute. I thought back to the pictures of Marina's first day of school. Zora had dressed her in what was formerly her favorite Moana T-shirt and a faded pair of jeans Zora's sister Leah had given us after Leah's daughter had grown out of hers. Zora never blamed me for not being there, but I still blamed myself, sometimes.

Kim coughed quietly on the couch, and then harder. "Fuck," she whispered after a minute.

"You okay?"

Kim kept her eyes closed. "I feel like death."

I got up and got her a glass of water, then went into the bathroom to find a thermometer. How did they only have those ear ones? Did those even work?

"Use this," I said, walking back into the living room and handing it to Kim. "Do you have anything with electrolytes?"

"There's, uh, that blue crap your daughter likes in the fridge."

I opened the fridge and moved the giant vat of soup Terry's dad had made when he visited to the side. "Gatorade?" Behind the Gatorade, more soup. Arroz Caldo. Squash.

"Sure."

"You keep this here for Marina?" I asked, smiling.

Kim coughed again. "It's 102," she choked.

I turned around. "That's high. Maybe we should go to the hospital."

"Your brain doesn't get to melty until, like, 105 or something," she said.

"Very scientific." I brought the Gatorade over, and a damp cloth from the kitchen, one with chickens on it. I passed the cloth and sat on the chair. "We're not waiting for your brain to melt." I took the thermometer from her. "It's 102.4," I said.

"Same thing." She started coughing and took a drink from the glass I'd put next to the soup bowl. She made a face. "That shit's gross."

"Not the same. We should go to the hospital."

"I'll go in another degree," Kim said. "If it hits 103.5, I won't argue."

"Kim, this is serious."

"So am I. I promise, 103.5."

I rolled my eyes. "How about 103?"

"Fine," she said, and immediately started coughing again. I moved next to her and pressed the cool cloth—a wedding present from Terry's parents that Kim thought ridiculous, I remembered—to her forehead. I sat there and rubbed her back until she fell asleep.

I didn't remember closing my eyes, but I must have, because when I opened them again two hours had passed. I looked down at Kim, her head in my lap, her skin pale and breathing shallow. When I checked again, she had a fever of 103.1.

Gently, I moved Kim's head and slid out from under her to call Terry.

"Sadie?" His voice was thick with sleep. I hadn't even remembered the time difference.

"Sorry—I didn't mean to wake you," I said. I bit my lip and looked back at Kim.

"No, it's okay. What's going on?"

"I'm taking Kim to the hospital," I said. "She's really sick."

There was silence on his end. And then, "I'm coming home."

"Terry—"

"No, I shouldn't have left. I'm getting on the next flight."

"Zora can pick you up at the airport." I couldn't imagine her saying no.

"Thank God for you both," he said. "What about Marina?"

"Zora's parents are around."

"Okay. Okay—I'll let you know as soon as I find out when I'm coming in. There's a bag in our closet with clothes and stuff in case—well, in case this happened."

"No problem."

The line went dead, and I went into the bedroom to grab Kim's cancer bag from the closet. When I came back into the living room, Kim was struggling to sit up on the couch, her eyes still half-closed. "Terry?"

My heart sank. Had we gotten to brain-melty already? "No, it's Sadie."

"Oh. Sadie—" she cut herself off when she started hacking up a lung into the chicken cloth, hunched over and struggling to breathe. I went over to her and put a hand on her shoulder for support, maybe for her and maybe for me. When she pulled the cloth away, there were small spots of blood between the cartoon birds. One of them had blood on its eye.

"We're going to the hospital," I said. "Can you stand?"

"Yeah," she wheezed, and nearly rolled off the couch. She made it as far as the chair before she stopped and sat down, out of breath.

I slipped my shoes on, grabbed Kim's keys, and rushed back. "You're going to lean on me, okay?" Without waiting for her to reply, I put her arm around my shoulders and half helped, half dragged Kim to the door. We made it as far as the porch when she broke away from me to lean against the railing, coughing up more blood onto Terry's garden below. She stopped for a moment to remember how to breathe again, and then reached for me. I helped her into her back seat, and then called Terry from the front.

"There's a flight in six hours," he said by way of greeting. "I'll be there by noon tomorrow."

"I'll tell Zora," I said, already pulling onto the highway. "We're five minutes out from General."

"Sadie are you sure, I mean, will you be okay? Going into the hospital?"

"I promise you: my dead son and suicide are the last thing on my mind right now."

"Just take care of yourself too."

"It's not even the same hospital."

"Promise me."

"Promise, promise." I knew I sounded dismissive, but really, it meant a lot to me that he remembered to care about me, that he and Kim had stood by me.

I could lose one of them today.

"Okay, I'll see you soon."

"Bye," I said as the line went dead. I wiped my eyes on the back of my hand and looked back at Kim in the rear-view mirror. Blood had tinted her lips red. She hadn't moved.

I'd been back at the hospital for two hours or so the next day when I heard Kim moan next to me. I put down the magazine I'd been reading and grabbed her hand. "Hey, you're okay. You're in the hospital."

Kim cracked one eye open. Someone had taken off the oxygen mask they'd put on when we'd come in, but she still had tubes going up her nose. Her left arm had three different bags of fluids going into one vein. "What happened?"

"Your brain got up to melty. You have pneumonia." I gave her a small smile. "Turns out weeks of chemo sucks for your immune system." Part of me was glad that Kim hadn't been awake when they told me the day before. I had broken down sobbing, sure that pneumonia at this stage was a death sentence. A far too kind nurse had to assure me that it wasn't.

Kim coughed weakly and sighed. "Who knew?" she deadpanned. "I mean, at least it's not the cancer." She took a deep breath. "Thanks for not letting me die I guess—" She cut herself off with more coughing.

"Stop talking."

She made a face and rolled her eyes. "I should to call Terry."

"He's on his way." I glanced up at the clock above the hospital bed. "Actually, he should be here any minute."

"Ugh. I feel bad." She choked on the last word and had to stop.

"I promise, he loves you more than he loves nerding out at some conference in Japan."

"Mmhmm." She closed her eyes. "I know."

We heard Terry before we saw him. Not yelling, exactly, but his voice louder than usual. I poked my head out of the door and called his name. "Terry!"

He and Zora turned around. The nurse at the desk behind them looked a little relieved, honestly. Terry ran toward me, Zora right behind him. I held the door open and he went right to Kim, sitting in the chair I'd just vacated. "Hi, baby." He grabbed her hand.

Kim smiled weakly up at Terry. "Hi."

"She's not supposed to talk much," I said. "But, of course, she can't stand not to sass me." Kim stuck her tongue out in my direction, and Zora stifled a laugh.

Terry turned back to us. "Thank you both for everything."

"Yeah, because you've never done anything for us," Zora said.

"Thanks again for not letting me die, Sade," Kim said. She coughed weakly into her hand and Terry brushed her hair back from her forehead.

"Anytime. We'll stop by tomorrow?"

Terry got up and gave us both hugs. "I'll keep you posted." When we left the room, Terry was already back by Kim's side, holding her right hand with both of his.

THE FOURTH LETTER:
WHEN I LOVED YOU

Dear Talia,

You had friends by the time we got to middle school, but I didn't. Not really. I sat at lunch with kids who didn't speak to me unless I spoke to them, and sometimes not even then. I'd traveled with them from our fifth-grade elementary school class and we just kind of stuck together, even though we had nothing in common. Over the course of middle and high school, we would all break off from our childhood friendships and find ones that made more sense. I was the first to sit elsewhere in the cafeteria.

But you noticed me anyway and thought that—for some reason still unknown to me—I was worth your time. You had asked me to sit with you at lunch. We had started sitting together in English, and I remember you as one of the only other students who didn't cry at the end of *Walk*

Two Moons by Sharon Creech, even though even the teacher cried.

We're past thirty now, and I still remember being eleven and sitting at one of the round tables in the corner of the middle school cafeteria. We talked books, mostly. All of us—you, me, and a handful of your friends from elementary school—had read *The Boxcar Children* and had fallen in love with the Alden children, especially fearless Jessie, though we both agreed that I was more like shy and sensitive Violet. I could have counted on one hand the times I had felt truly included until that moment. You gave me that.

We were the biggest literary nerds of our friends, which eventually expanded beyond the handful of us and became something like a real group. We all had things in common, but I enjoyed spending time with you and you alone, playing word games in your parents' living room and writing horror stories with twist endings in the margins of our notebooks in English and, later, in other classes.

I think I recognized when my liking you as a friend turned into a crush, but I didn't know what it meant. In truth, I had never crushed on anyone in real life before—not a character in a book or TV show, I mean—and hadn't fully accepted yet that I didn't think about men the way I thought about women. I pretended to myself that I had a crush on the boys in our classes, even though I never talked about them with anyone else. At sleepovers where most of our friends talked about the cute guys in gym, I just nodded along and pretended like I knew what they were talking about. When they asked me who I liked, I said, "No one." You were usually there, alert and ready to talk about whoever it was that had caught your eye, even though you told me privately that you didn't really care.

The first time I went into a psych hospital, it was the end of eighth grade, and I had attempted suicide for the first time. I waited until Kate and Aaron were out of the house, and slit my wrists in the bathtub. I have vague memories of Aaron screaming, of the ride to the hospital. It turns out, I had slit them the wrong way, and not deep enough to bleed out on time. I didn't tell you where I really was—I told you that my grandfather was sick, I think—but you knew. You never asked about it. I came close to telling you a few times, but you always changed the topic. Something about some boy or a party you wanted to go to.

By high school, I'd come out to a few of our friends—including you—but I never said anything about how you made me feel. You laughed at my not-often-funny jokes and read my stories when we took creative writing together in high school. You made the lining of my stomach flutter with proverbial butterflies. I didn't always know how to act around you, but you made it a little bit easier just by being.

Outside of us, you made it easier to be me too. We shared a locker room row in gym for four years in high school, after they made us change into T-shirts and shorts to play soccer or volleyball. I hated myself then, something I'm sure you knew early on. Thin slashes decorated my outer thighs over stretch marks where I had manifested my hatred of myself into something physical. But you being there, and me making you laugh at my not-funny jokes, I forgot how much I hated my body, a physical manifestation of my being. For a moment, I was just another person in the locker room, outside of my own head.

Do you remember the night we kissed? I had just turned twenty-one, and you, having done so the month prior, took me out. We went to a bar over fall break and did tequila shots, resulting in the worst hangover I'd had and have ever had. Before we stumbled home, you took my head in your hands and kissed me, fierce and possessive. When I asked you what that was for, momentarily sobered by your actions, you shrugged. "I just wanted to see what it was like," you said. I don't know if anything would have happened between us if I had been braver, but I don't think I want to.

That last year of college you came home with a boyfriend and more confidence. I pretended to be happy for you and gave you a hug hello. Honestly though, I'm glad this all happened when it did because if it hadn't, I might have been waiting on you, and I might never have spoken to Zora.

Zora doesn't know how upset I was when you RSVP'd no to our wedding. No explanation, no excuse. Aaron is the only one I said something to, and he asked me how I felt about it. I told him I was okay, and he said, "I'd be really angry." I wasn't angry. Just hurt. Maybe that's not fair to you, but I would have liked to know why, or at least have heard from you that you still cared.

I don't know what our relationship will look like moving forward, if it's sustainable. You never came to see me in the psych hospital, and that hurt more than I'll admit to Zora. I know it was far from Long Island, but it wasn't so much, really. Not if you had wanted to come.

I can honestly say I'm happier with Zora than I ever would have been with you. Mine and Zora's is a quiet love, one that works without screaming fights and questioning everything about us all the time. I didn't fully understand how my heart could expand for Marina until she came to exist. My life is one I never thought I'd lead, and even though I tried to end it, I'm realizing I couldn't be happier any other way. Still, I can't help wonder sometimes what would have happened if something had happened between us. Probably nothing good.

Love (even when inconvenient),

Sadie

NIGHTMARES

The school had tried Zora first. When they couldn't reach her at work, they called me. I walked in on Marina sitting on a chair in the principal's office with her arms crossed, kicking her legs. I knelt in front of her. "What happened, Bunny?"

"Leslie said you weren't a good mom. So I punched her."

My gut twisted. Leslie Rogers and Marina had been close since preschool. We used to carpool with her parents. "Why did she say that?"

Marina shrugged. "She said that her mom said. . ." She trailed off and stared at her knees, lightly scarred from half a dozen falls on the playground.

"You know that punching Leslie was wrong though, right?" Marina shrugged, and I said, "Marina, I need you to tell me you know that punching Leslie was a bad thing to do."

"I know." She still wouldn't look at me.

I turned back to the principal. "Can I take her home?" Principal Franklin nodded and I took Marina's hand.

We stopped at the park on the way home. I got Marina an ice cream cone and we sat on a bench by a running path. "Marina, can you tell me why you got so upset with Leslie today?"

"I told you. She called you a bad mom."

"I know, sweetheart. But why did that bother you so much?"

Marina looked up at me, frowning. "Because she doesn't get to."

"Well, next time, what can we do instead?"

Marina sighed. "Use my words."

"And what can we say to Leslie?"

"That's not nice."

"Awesome." I raised my hand, and she gave me a high-five, her fingers sticky with chocolate.

She licked her cone and looked around. "I don't think you're a bad mom," she said. "I just wish you didn't have to go away."

My heart nearly stopped. "Me too, baby. But I'm back now. And I'm here to love you and lecture you and do all the mom things. Okay?"

"Hmm. . ." She raised her sticky fingers to her chin, thinking. "Maybe not lecture."

"Sorry, kiddo. It's part of the job."

"Fine, I guess." She took another lick and stood up. "Can we go to the playground?"

"How about this weekend?"

She tilted her head, considering it. Then she stuck out

her hand. "Deal." We shook on it.

***

Zora knocked so softly on the open bedroom door I wouldn't have heard, except that my music happened to stop at just the right moment. I took my headphones out. "You don't have to knock. It's your room too."

"Can we talk?" she asked. Her eyes were red-rimmed and swollen.

"Yeah, of course," I said, and moved to the bed.

She sat next to me. "Terry came by today," she said. "Before you came home with Marina from the park."

"Is Kim okay?"

"No worse than she's been," she said. "She's just sleeping a lot. Recovering from the hospital." She picked at the skin around her nail and said, "We talked. For a long time, actually. He cried a lot. He said—he said he didn't know how he was supposed to watch his wife die."

"She might not die," I said.

"Sadie, she's not doing well," Zora said. "He just doesn't. . . He wants her not to be sick. But that isn't going to happen." A tear slipped down her cheek. She kept her eyes on her hands in her lap. She reminded me of Marina.

My breath caught and I felt tears welling up in my own eyes. "Why are you telling me this?" I asked.

Zora turned and looked at me, finally. "We talked for a long time and I think I realized a lot of his feelings are feelings I might have, well, had. No, I know they are. About when you went into the hospital. And I know it isn't fair, and I love you so much. You have to know how much I love you. There were just days when it was really hard and—I feel like such a shitty fucking person for feeling like this. For having felt like this." She stopped for a moment to wipe her eyes on her sleeve. I was crying now too.

"It's not your fault," I said, because I didn't know what else to say.

"I know. But it's not yours either, which is what makes it so—" She shook her head, her lips turned in a deep frown, and started over. "If there were someone I could blame, you know? I never thought about not wanting to be with you, of course. I just thought about what it might be like if—"

"If I never got sick," I said.

"Yeah. Exactly." She blinked back another wave of tears. "But you have to know, I'd never trade a day of sick you for a healthy someone else."

"I know," I said, offering her a small smile. "It sucks to hear this, but. . . I'm glad you told me."

Zora sighed and took my hand. She put her head on my shoulder and pulled herself closer to me, so that her legs crossed over mine. "I've been thinking, maybe I could start seeing someone too? For therapy?"

"I really like that idea," I said, and held her tighter. "At least to try it."

"Maybe. . . Could you see if Rosa knows anyone?"

"Of course."

"Moms!"

Zora sat up and we both turned to the doorway. Marina stood there in her Coco pajamas, her hair sticking up at odd angles.

"What's going on, Bunny?" I asked.

"I had a bad dream," Marina said, her lip trembling. "Can I sleep here?"

"Of course," Zora said, scooping her up.

Marina pressed her hand to Zora's cheek, still damp. "Did you have a bad dream too, Mama?"

"Mmhmm. But now you and your other mom are here and everything is okay," she said, shooting me a wink. She put Marina down in our bed and I crawled in next to her. I fell asleep holding my wife and daughter in my arms.

***

Kim nearly drifted off at the table more than once, but she insisted on being there for her weekly diner date with Rodney. "You should come," she had told me, and so I did. I liked Rodney, but really I went because I thought Kim might crash the car if I let her drive on her own. When her head drifted onto my shoulder for a third time at the table, she snapped to attention, startled.

"She's stubborn," Rodney said to me. "I told her we didn't have to do this while she was recovering from freaking pneumonia."

"It's tradition," Kim mumbled, blinking her eyes open.

"You can't talk her out of anything once she's made up her mind," I said. "I've tried."

Kim shrugged and took a sip of her coffee, black. Rodney flattened part of his BLT with his fork. "What do you do, Sadie?"

"I'm a writer," I said. "I'm working part-time right now. At a library." I glanced over at Kim, who nodded. I took a breath and said, "I taught creative writing, but I went into inpatient treatment last year for. . . depression."

Rodney nodded. "Nothing more depressing than being locked up for depression."

Kim laughed. My heart stopped pounding and I let myself smile.

The waitress came over with a dessert menu and glanced at the table, the half-eaten sandwich on Rodney's plate and the half-drunk coffee in front of Kim. I was the only one who had finished my salad. "Can I get you anything else?" she asked.

"Just the check, please," Rodney said. "I'll take this to go."

She took the sandwich and my plate. Rodney waited until she was gone before he said, "I had to do something like that once. The first time I had cancer I ended up addicted to morphine." He shuddered. "Almost worse than the disease."

"You went to rehab?" I asked.

"Mmhmm. Shaking and hot flashes and all that. Yeah." He nodded and said, "You can die from too much of that shit. Your heart stops and you just don't wake up."

"I'm sorry."

Rodney snorted. "What for? You didn't give me too much morphine."

"Sadie apologizes too much," Kim said. "It's her least attractive quality." She and Rodney both laughed and, against my every instinct, I laughed with them.

The waitress came by with the check and the sandwich. Rodney grabbed the check. "My turn," he said.

"I can pay for mine," I protested.

"You'll pay next time," Rodney said.

"If there is a next time," Kim said. She put her head against the wall and closed her eyes. Since the pneumonia, she'd lost more weight. She was paler too, as though she hadn't seen the sun in weeks.

I tore my eyes away from her face and looked back at Rodney. "Sounds good," I said.

***

High school is hard, but not all of it is painful. You don't have real dates to the senior prom, so you go with friends, a group of misfits collected through the years. Talia wears yellow, a color you didn't even know you liked until you see her in it. Later, you will remember her hair down and the way the dress twists around her shoulders at the top. You wear purple that night, a color across on the wheel you had studied in art class.

The music is nearly just as loud on the first floor as it is on the second, where the real party is. You and several of your friends sneak away and claim your space, dancing wildly where no one watches. You run across the linoleum tiles and yell the lyrics to overplayed pop songs as they come on over the loud speakers. You dance together with your hands clumsily placed on the other's body, one of yours on a hip and one on a shoulder. You scream Avril Lavigne and Jimmy Eat World in each other's faces until your lungs give out.

Later, you take a car to Brighton Beach and watch the sun rise over the water. You sit back against the sand and soak it in, a moment on the razor-thin edge between childhood and the real world. You lay your head in a friend's lap while some of the others dance on the shore to no music, just off-key lyrics they belt themselves. When you eventually go back to the psych hospital, not one of these friends will visit.

***

When I tried to talk about something serious, Talia wouldn't answer my texts. When I asked her about our friendship over the phone, she would suddenly have to go. Finally, we met in person, at her house on Long Island. She'd tried to serve us wine, until I reminded her that I wasn't supposed to drink on my meds. She made tea instead.

"Chamomile or vanilla?"

"Chamomile," I said. When she sat down again I asked, "How are things?"

"You know. Busy, busy." She sat down with two mugs and said, "I might be up for a promotion, actually."

"That's amazing."

"Yeah, I'm excited about it," she said.

"How are things with Mark?" I asked. Most nights, she stayed at his place. She'd let me know how special it was that she'd stayed home for me.

She looked around, as though he might appear from the shadows at any moment. Finally, she leaned forward and whispered, "I think he's going to propose."

"Oh, wow! Are you— Would you say yes?"

"Yes, of course. I'm really happy."

I waited, but she never asked me about my life. I sipped my tea as she went on about Mark's parents and how they really loved her and how of course they would live here but maybe get married in California because that's where he's from. . .

"That's really great."

"Yeah, so, anyway." She shrugged.

"I'm happy for you, Tal."

"And you'll be in the wedding party, of course," she added, as though just remembering that I was in the room.

"Oh. I will?"

"Yes, of course! Why wouldn't you be?"

"You didn't even come to my wedding."

Talia froze, like she had forgotten and was trying to recall that hazy time in her life during which I'd been happy. "Oh, I couldn't. You remember."

"No, actually, you never told me why you didn't come."

The pause between us should have made me uncomfortable. I found myself maintaining eye contact, even when Talia tried to pull away. After a minute she said, "I didn't?"

"No. You didn't."

"Oh. I'm sorry."

"Yeah, it kind of hurt."

"Well. . . That's all in the past though, right?"

"Actually, not really." I shifted on the couch, so that I was facing her directly. "Why didn't you come see me in the psych hospital?"

"I told you, it was really hard—"

"You know what, it was harder on me," I said. "And Zora. And other people who love me."

"I know that—"

"My friend Kim has cancer," I said. "She's dying, and she still makes time for me. She asks me how I am and actually cares about the answer. She stops me when I tell her everything is okay and makes me tell her the truth because I matter to her."

"You matter to me! How could you even say that?"

"Because you haven't shown it. Talia, it didn't even occur to me that I would be in your wedding party."

"You're one of my best friends. Of course—"

"No, you don't get to make excuses anymore," I said. "I'm done with that."

"Sadie, what are you saying?"

"I'm saying I'm done making time for you if you won't make time for me. Do you realize I've been here for an hour and you never once asked me how I am?" I paused, waiting for her to answer. When she didn't, I said, "That's because you're happy. And you don't want to talk about things that aren't happy."

Talia snarled, her face turning ugly. "Fuck you."

"Fine." I stood and grabbed my bag. "I hope it's a beautiful wedding."

I stormed out of Talia's house and slammed the car door. I sat behind the wheel, breathing heavily, processing. She was my best friend, the only person that really understood me for so many years. But this wasn't high school anymore, and I wasn't the same person. She wasn't really, either. And whoever she had become wasn't who I needed in the life I'd made.

When I'd realized what I'd done, what this meant for me, my heart soared, and I smiled.

STUPID THINGS

Rosa put her pen and pad on her desk and looked at me over her glasses. "You know, you'd be a terrible poker player."

I laughed. "What does that even mean?"

"It means you have the same damn look on your face when something is bothering you," she said. "It's your tell."

"Do you play a lot of poker, then?" I teased.

"Do you need to know the answer to that?" she asked. Every time I asked her a question about her personal life, that was the response. 'Why do you need to know that, Sadie?' 'We're not here to discuss me, Sadie.'

"No," I said. "It wouldn't hurt me, though." I used to have a therapist that would tell me all about her daughter. Every session, I'd come in and let her do so for forty-five minutes. After four months, she realized she'd made no progress and told Kate it wasn't working out.

"What's on your mind?"

"Zora wants a referral," I said. "For a therapist."

"I can give her one."

"I know." I picked at the bottom of my skirt, then smoothed it out. It was getting warmer outside.

"And that's bothering you because. . ."

"It's bothering me because it's, well, not bothering me," I said. I moved my hands back to my lap and twisted my wedding ring. "She was really upset. No, not upset. We had a really good talk and she told me about how she felt after I tried to kill myself. It was hard to hear, but. . . I'm glad she told me."

"Why do you think that needs to bother you?"

"Because I really hurt her," I said. "She wants professional help."

"So? You're getting professional help."

"Zora isn't like me," I said.

"What?" Rosa asked. "Human?"

"Broken."

"Therapy doesn't mean you're broken." She picked up her pad and waved it at me. "It just means you might need a little help being whole."

***

Kim wasn't supposed to run (as per doctor's orders) and it drove her nuts. "Just let me do one lap." She reached up and pulled her ponytail tighter. She was sitting, but her feet were already on the ground and poised to go.

I rolled my eyes. We were on the bench closest to the park entrance by Kim and Terry's house, by the lake. "I'm not your mom."

"Fine." She hopped up off the bench and stumbled forward a bit. I reached out to steady her, and she bat my hand away. "I'm fine."

"Is there something you want to talk about?" I asked. "Because I don't think my hand did anything to you."

She crossed her arms and kicked a rock, avoiding my gaze. "We had a fight last night."

"Who? You and Terry?"

"Yeah."

"What about?"

"Stupid things," she spat.

"Stupid things like. . ."

She sat again and put her feet up on the bench, hugging her knees to her chest. "After he came home from Japan, I told him he didn't need to come back just because I was sick." She sighed. "He brought it up again last night. He said of course he had to come. Otherwise he'd just be freaking out the whole time he was over there. I told him to stop and he snapped and said I didn't know what he was going through." She took a breath. "He apologized right away. I said if he was so upset than maybe it would be better if he didn't have to go through this." She closed her eyes, tight. "I said I wished he'd never loved me."

I bit my lip. What do you say to that?

Kim looked up at me. "I told him it would be easier for him if he never loved me. I was screaming it at him, and of course he was being his stupid calm self. He kept apologizing and trying to get near me but I told him I needed space."

"Jeez."

"Yeah. He went out for a drive. I don't know where." We stared out at the lake for a while, not saying anything.

After a while, Kim said, "It's stupid. I don't want him to not. . . I hate feeling like I'm responsible for what he's going through. Honestly, it would be easier for me if I didn't have to worry about him too."

"In some ways," I said. "In some ways, it would be so much harder."

"You're right. I know that." She dug her nails into her sleeve and held on tight. "I pretended to be sleeping when he left for work this morning."

"So you haven't seen him since—"

She shook her head. "I just needed some space." She put her head down onto her knees and cried.

We walked for a bit. A shorter route, just half a mile. Then we made our way back to the house. Terry's car was there when we walked up the driveway, and the door was open when we walked in.

"Terry?"

Terry came running from down the hall. He paused, unsure if he should wait for her to come to him. When she did, he put his arms around her and held on for dear life, his and hers.

"I'm so sorry. I didn't mean it." She apologized over and over again, her face buried in his shoulder and her voice muffled by the sleeve of his Princeton Hospital T-shirt.

"I know that. I know. I'm sorry too." Terry made eye contact with me and mouthed 'Thank you.' I gave him a smile and a nod, and backed out onto the porch. I shut the door behind me.

I was about to call a Lyft when Terry opened the door. "Let me drive you."

"I'm fine."

"Really. It'll take me ten minutes."

"Only if you're sure –"

"C'mon." He took his keys and unlocked the doors. I slid into the passenger's side and Terry started the car. After a minute of driving he said, "I don't know what she told you but. . . you should know that none of it was her fault."

I turned to him, startled. "It wasn't anyone's fault."

"She's going through so much. I shouldn't have said. . . Anyway, thanks."

"For what?"

Terry shrugged. "For being there, I guess. For being a friend."

I actually laughed. "Terry, have you ever met my friend Talia?" He shook his head and I said, "She was my best friend in high school. We were still close, when I got pregnant with Asher. She never once came and saw me in the psych hospital." His eyes were on the road, but the muscles in his face had tensed. "What I'm trying to say is, you don't need to thank me. This is what we do."

"Well. Then I'm glad for that."

"Me too."

Another pause. "Do. . . You don't think I'm awful? For saying—"

"Terry, it sucks. This whole thing sucks. It sucks worse for Kim. But that doesn't mean you aren't allowed to be overwhelmed sometimes. And say the wrong thing."

"Yeah." He pulled into the train station and turned to look at me. His eyes sparkled with tears. "I'm scared, Sadie."

I bit my lip. Twisted my wedding ring around my finger. "I know," I said. "I'm scared too."

***

Zora stayed behind from Aaron's set one night with Marina, so I went alone. "You can call Kim and Terry," she said before I left.

I shook my head. "I checked on her before. She's. . . tired." I glanced over at Marina. Truthfully, she'd been in bed with a major migraine all day, but I couldn't go into specifics when Marina wasn't around.

Zora understood and kissed me on the cheek. "Tell Aaron I send my congrats," she said.

After the set, when Aaron finished playing two whole encores, he came and sat with me at the bar.

"You were awesome."

He grinned. "Thanks, Sade." His eyeliner bled a bit around his eyes and beads of sweat stood out against his forehead. He looked like he had just run a marathon, and happened to smash his previous record in the process. The bartender came over and Aaron said, "Water, please."

"You don't have to not drink just because I'm not drinking." I held up my mocktail to emphasize the point.

"Nah. Water's just free." The bartender set a glass down and Aaron said, "Thanks, man." He took a sip and said, "So I have something to tell you. You can't tell Mom yet."

"Half the things I say to Kate are lies anyway," I said. "Spill."

Aaron laughed. "You really inspire me to confide in you."

"Shut up and tell me."

"I got in touch with my foster family," he said. "The

couple that had me for a few months in Seoul before I was adopted."

"That's amazing!"

"I'm really happy," he said. "Apparently they had this huge party for me on my hundredth day. It's a big thing in South Korea. They sent pictures."

"Do you have them?"

He pulled his phone out and handed it to me. Baby Aaron had his eyes closed in this photo, and he was surrounded by presents. Most of them were wrapped, some of them half-way. He sat in someone's lap, someone wearing jeans and a white sweater. He wore a pale green T-shirt and tiny jeans.

I swiped. This was Aaron, his eyes wide open, and another child. This kid was maybe two years old and wearing a party hat. "Who's that?"

"That's Dae. She was the couple's biological daughter. Apparently we were super close."

I handed the phone back to him. "Do they speak English?"

"Pretty well. They invited me to come visit. I'm just not sure I'm ready for that yet."

"Whatever you do, I'm really happy for you."

He smiled again, wide. "Thanks." He looked just past me and his eyes lit up. "Lily!"

Lily with the pink hair and the moon tattoo appeared at my shoulder. "You did so good, Aaron," she said. She looked at me. "Is this your sister?"

I stuck out my hand. "Sadie." She shook it.

"Lily and I were going to get a bite," Aaron said. "Come with?"

I looked back and forth between them. "I've gotta get

home, actually. Back to Zora and Marina."

Aaron hugged me, and I grabbed my bag. "Thanks for coming."

"Of course. It was great to meet you, Lily."

I left the bar, turning back at the door. Aaron was laughing at something Lily had said, his hand on her arm. I smiled and walked out.

***

The two of you have been dating for six months when Zora asks you what you would do if you didn't write or teach. You tell her you can't imagine anything else for yourself.

"Oh, c'mon. You must have a single other interest."

Don't laugh. When I was a kid, I thought I wanted to be a vet, and then I realized, well, science.

"I'm not laughing." The two of you sit in Zora's apartment. She shares it with two other med school students, constantly running in and out with lab coats and backpacks that must weigh at least as much as a small child.

I didn't want to kill a sick dog, either.

Zora laughs. "That's fair. I don't think that would bother me too much, if I knew it was the right thing to do. But it would be sad."

What about you? you ask her. If you weren't going to be a doctor.

"I'd want to work with kids," she said. "I don't know about teaching, but something with kids."

I can see that, you say. You'd be good at that.

Zora sits up and mock-bows. "Why thank you," she says.

Do you want kids?
She nods, suddenly serious. "I do."
Me too, you say.

THE FIFTH LETTER:
TO WHOEVER YOU ARE

Dear. . .

It's hard to write a letter when you're not entirely sure who you're addressing. You're not my mother. That position belongs to Kate and Kate only. I suppose you're my birth mother, but that still feels a bit strange. You're not entirely a stranger, since we knew each other once, and intimately. I grew inside you for nine months and brought you brutal pain when I came into the world. I know that because I've given birth.

I don't remember ever not knowing I was adopted. It was always something we talked about, me and Kate and even my adoptive father, who left when I was nine. I was only two when we brought Aaron home, but I must have known Kate wasn't pregnant like so many of my friend's parents had been preceding the birth of a younger sibling.

Adoption was never taboo, never something to be ashamed of. Kate got a lot wrong, but she also got a lot right, and that was one of those things.

There are a lot of things about being adopted I didn't realize would affect me, or have affected me as profoundly as they have. Growing up, many of my peers assumed I was white, until they met my brother Aaron, who is Korean. Especially going to temple in Brooklyn, where there were no Latinas for me to identify with. Kate always told me I was Latina and tried to explain it the best she could, having grown up in white suburbia with little to no knowledge about what that actually meant.

For people who knew, they were always astounded to learn I didn't speak Spanish. I took six years of the language in middle and high school, but it was embarrassing to be the Latina struggling to roll her Rs. Worse was when those same people would ask me where I was from—I knew they weren't asking about New York—and I had to tell them I didn't know. My family's history extends to Austria, Germany, and Italy, but biologically I am something entirely different. I just don't know what.

There are so many questions I wish I could have asked you when I was pregnant with Asher. Did you crave eggs like I did? Did you feel me dancing in your stomach like I felt Asher? Did you love me then? I'm not sure how I could have given up Asher, but it has made me think a lot about what you did. I'm not angry, and I never have been. It's just made me think a lot about what you must have gone through, the decision you had to make. I will never know why, and I think I'm okay with that.

I did wonder in the psych hospital if you would have come to visit me. I tell myself it doesn't matter, that I have a family, but eventually I had to admit that I did feel your absence with me as I sought to make myself whole. With me as I slept in a bed with scratchy hospital sheets and when I ate overcooked eggs in the cafeteria crowded with patients I never spoke to. The void was terribly suffocating and lonely.

I didn't realize until after Asher, until after I left the psych hospital and started seeing Rosa, that part of why I wanted to get pregnant was so there would be someone in this world I could have that biological connection to. I'm still not sure why I thought I needed that, but I am starting to understand the urge. It's a pull I can't entirely put into words, but I have been trying to.

There are questions I want to ask you regardless, basic ones. Do you prefer red wine or white? Who are your favorite authors? Do you have any other biological children? The thing is, though, that I am not curious enough to come looking for you. I've spoken about this with Aaron, who feels very differently. What if he has other siblings out there somewhere? What if his birth parents actually want to meet him? None of this is sufficient reason for me to want you in my life. You will always be part of my story, but I don't feel a need to give you a larger role.

I don't know why you gave me up. If you had to, if you weren't ready. I don't know what you want to hear about me. Would you want to know about Kate, about our antagonism, and about how much I love her? Would you want to hear about Aaron and how he's not only my brother but one of my closest friends? Would you be delighted to hear that I'm a mother through adoption or dismayed to hear about my sordid mental health history?

These are questions I will never know the answer to,

and I am okay not knowing. Maybe we will meet one day, and more likely, we won't. Either way, I hope that wherever you are, you are happy.

From,
Sadie

THE GOOD AND THE BAD

"You must be married."

No. You tell her you aren't married.

"A serial killer then. Or just a regular killer. Or an anti-vaxxer."

No, no, no.

Zora sips her drink. "There must be something wrong with you," she says.

And why is that?

"Because you're perfect."

You blush. You don't blush easily, even though you embarrass often. But this woman you've known for a night makes you feel like a princess in a cartoon. Fragile and lucky. Your first date is to the Cubbyhole, a famous lesbian bar in Manhattan. The bar smells like bodies and beer, but when Zora leans close to you, you smell her: sweet sweat and some kind of floral shampoo.

It is late when the two of you leave, but when Zora asks

you if you want to take a walk, you say yes. The air is crisp with changing seasons and dead leaves crunch under your feet. You talk about all the things that might make you not-perfect. You are Latina, but you do not speak Spanish.

"So? No one thinks I speak Spanish because I'm black. My mom is from El Salvador. I'm fluent."

You're an. . . anxious person.

"And?"

You don't have the best relationship with your parents. Zora laughs. "I don't know many queer people who do."

She kisses you for the first time by Central Park, catching you by surprise. Her lips are soft and her hands are warm on your cheeks. She pulls away and tucks her hair behind her ear. "Was that okay?"

As an answer, you kiss her back.

"Homework?"

I rolled my eyes at Kim, hooked up to her IV at chemo. She had finally convinced Terry not to take off work for her appointment on the condition that I could drive her home.

"Want to talk about it?" she asked.

"It's nothing, really. Just, writing helps me remember."

"The bad stuff?"

I glanced down at what I'd written and closed my laptop. "The good stuff too."

"Good," she said.

I looked around the room. There was a woman I recognized two chairs down, who had lost most of her hair since Kim had started. In the chair beside that woman, an older man I'd never seen sat with two young women that shared his sloping nose and ginger hair. Beside him—my stomach lurched—a young girl holding a stuffed bear in one hand and a woman's hand in the other. The chair next to Kim was empty.

"Did I miss Rodney?" I asked. He usually left about halfway through Kim's appointment, but I hadn't come that late.

Kim looked away. "Rodney died," she said. "A nurse told me when I got here."

"Shit. I'm sorry."

Kim exhaled through her nose and turned back to me. "Thanks," she said.

A nurse approached the young girl at the end of the row and seemed to ask her a question because the girl shook her head 'no.' Kim glanced over at her too. Her eyes scanned the girl's dark hair, her Tweety Bird T-shirt. "That's Amy," she said. "She came for the first time last time I was here."

"Is she going to die?" I asked, lowering my voice.

Kim laughed, but it was hollow, almost haunting, and the maniacal grin on her face contrasted starkly with her wide eyes. She looked almost afraid. "We all are," she said.

On the way home, Kim cracked the window and leaned her head against the glass.

"You okay?"

"Just nauseous."

I glanced over at Kim in the passenger's seat. She had her eyes closed. "We're almost there."

"I won't throw up in your car," she said. True to her word, she waited until we pulled up to the house and ran out onto the lawn while the car was still on. She put a hand on the side of the house and leaned over, gagging. I shut the engine off, came up behind her, and held her hair back until she was done. One of Kim's neighbors watched from his porch.

She fumbled with her keys, unlocked her front door, and stumbled to the bathroom where she crouched in front of the toilet and promptly threw up again. Finally, she spat the taste of bile out into the toilet and sat back on her knees. "Ugh."

"Do you usually get sick like this?" I asked, pulling her hair back into the black band I kept on my wrist. Several strands fell onto my fingers. I brushed them away.

"Only last time," she said. I couldn't be at the last chemo appointment, but Terry had wanted to be there anyway. It was his birthday, and he wanted to spend it with his wife, wherever they were. Apparently, that place had ended up being the bathroom floor. "I usually don't feel well, but—" She went quiet and bent over the toilet again, gagging. She took a few deep breaths and said, "You don't have to sit here and watch me throw up."

"I'm a mom," I said. "You'll have to try harder to gross me out."

"The things you must have seen," she said. She gripped the sides of the toilet and retched again twice.

"Can I get you anything?" I put a hand on her shoulder.

Kim shook her head and flushed the toilet. "No," she gasped. Breathe in, then out.

You are lying together in bed when Zora says, "Let's get married."

You blink. What?

Your hands are laced together, fingers overlapping. "You heard me. Let's get married."

Really?

"Really, really." *Zora laughs.* "I love you. Marry me."

Yeah. Yeah, okay.

Zora grins and kisses you. You laugh, her mouth still on yours. Your thighs are still sore from earlier that evening, but you kiss her back, harder, and move to be on top.

I glanced at the time and shut my laptop. Kim looked over at me, turning the volume down on the TV. "You're leaving?"

"Not yet." Her face was still flushed and her hands shook just enough to be noticeable. "How are you feeling?"

"You sound like Terry."

"Oh no," I deadpanned. "The horror."

"I'm okay," she said. "Just tired."

"Can I get you anything?"

She shook her head. "No point."

"What do you mean?" She shrugged, and I moved to sit next to her. "Kim?" I took the remote from her hand and shut off the TV.

She leaned against the back of the couch so that her head touched the wall. "It just feels like a losing battle this time." She shrugged again and said, "I'm just so tired." A tear snaked its way down her cheek and I wiped it away.

I hesitated. "Maybe you should be seeing someone?"

"Like an affair? I know cancer-chic is very sexy, but I have to tell you I'm pretty in love with my husband."

"You know what I mean."

She smiled a lopsided, half-hearted smile and said, "I don't know. I kind of, you know, just want to spend time with Terry and you and Zora and my family here."

Before she dies. The thought burrowed its way into my

brain and I chased it out again. I put a hand on her leg, squeezed, and said, "Whatever you need. Okay?"

"Okay." She put her hand on top of mine, steadying it somewhat. "Thanks, Sadie."

The front door opened and Kim furiously wiped at her eyes before Terry saw her tears. Terry kicked off his shoes and sat on the arm of the couch by Kim's head. "How was it?" He still had his keys in his hand.

"It was a party," Kim said. "Me and all the other chemo kids."

Terry looked at me. "Sadie?"

"She did great," I said. "She did get sick after."

"Hungover from all that partying."

He put a hand on her shoulder. "You, shush."

"I threw up on your flowers," she said. "Sorry."

"The flowers will be okay. There's worse stuff in fertilizer." He squeezed her shoulder and smiled at me. "Thank you."

"Literally, anytime," I said. I glanced at the clock on the wall and said, "I have to get Marina." To Kim, "Will you be okay?"

She waved a hand, dismissive. "I won't die today," she said.

"You're an asshole."

"I try my best."

"Really. I can ask Zora's mom to get her." I stowed my laptop in my bag. "Or Aaron."

"I'm fine. Terry will make sure. Go be with your daughter." Terry kept both eyes on her as she got up off the couch and gave me a hug goodbye. Her hands felt like ice on my back. She had just promised me she wouldn't die that day, but a tiny part of my brain always thought this might be the last time we see each other.

***

"Mom? Will you be here when I start first grade?"

I glanced at the rearview mirror. Marina finished Kindergarten next week, and then it was on to summer, sans karate. She met my eyes.

"Of course I will be."

"Oh. I just didn't know if you would go away again."

Deep breath. "No, Bunny. I was very sick last year, but I'm doing better now."

"Sick like Auntie Kim is sick?" she asked.

"Kind of, but not really."

"That doesn't make sense."

I hesitated, trying to find the right words. "I was. . . sick in my mind. It made me do things, like try to hurt myself, even though I know that's wrong. Auntie Kim is sick because there's something bad in her body trying to hurt her, and she's trying to fight it."

"Are you going to get sick again ever?"

I pulled up into a parking spot and looked back at Marina. "I hope not. You know how I'm going to therapy now?" Marina nodded, and I said, "That's to help me stay well."

Marina bit her lip. She looked less like Zora's double in that moment than ever before. In that moment, in fact, she reminded me of me. "It was really scary when you were gone, Mommy."

I blinked back tears and reached out for her hand. She let me take it. "For me too, Bunny."

***

"This is silly."

Rosa cracked one eye open. We were sitting on purple mats, both in short sleeves and yoga pants. "Your eyes are supposed to be closed."

"So are yours."

Rosa exhaled and closed both eyes again. "We're trying something."

I sighed. Audibly.

"Sadie. Are your eyes closed?"

I closed my eyes. "Yes."

"Good. Listen to the audio." Soft acoustics played from Rosa's laptop, and I tried to focus on the individual guitar strings, the humming of the instruments coming together. Was my breathing too fast? Did I always breathe this fast?

"Are you listening?"

"Yeah."

"Good. Let go of the stress of the week." I tried. Really. But to let go of this week, I had to let it pass through my head. And that's where everything—Rodney dying, Kim falling apart, Marina's questions—got stuck. I stood.

"Sadie?"

"I don't want to do this anymore."

Rosa opened her eyes. "Are you okay?"

"It's just a lot of alone time. With me. And my thoughts."

"Okay. That's fine." She reached up onto her desk and shut the music off. Then she gestured to the mat I'd vacated. I sat again, my knees to my chest. "Any particular thoughts overwhelming you?" I shrugged, and Rosa said,

"Just a whole week's worth?"

"It's gotten a lot easier," I said. "It's still not completely easy."

"Fair."

I dug my heels into the mat. It left a checked pattern on the bottom of my foot. "I'm going to let Kate meet Marina."

"That's a big step."

"You're really good at that, you know? Nothing is ever 'good' or 'bad.' Just 'a big step' or 'a lot' or. . . yeah."

"That is the first thing they teach us in therapy school," Rosa deadpanned. "To refer to things as just 'yeah.'"

"It's probably good," I said. "That's what I keep telling myself."

"What are you worried about?"

"Not Marina, so much," I said. "She's. . ." I grinned in spite of myself. "She's amazing. Whatever happens, she'll be fine."

"Whatever happens, you'll be fine too," Rosa said. "Nothing Kate says can change that."

"I hope so," I said. I tilted my feet forward, burying my toes in the squish of the yoga mat.

THUNDER

The day I finally let Kate see Marina, Zora took work off. "You need me," she said. "And Marina might need us both."

We'd told Marina that her other grandmother was coming, but she was still confused. When we told her she'd met Kate once before, just after she was adopted, Marina said, "Oh. That lady." Nothing else.

Kate made a beeline for Marina when she came, stopping only short of touching her. Zora had Marina on her lap.

"Hi, Marina. I'm your grandma."

"I already have a grandma," she said.

"Your other grandma."

Marina shrugged. "Okay." She looked up at Zora. "Can I go now?"

Zora looked over at me, and so did Marina. "You can go," I said. Marina took off running, ignoring Kate's frown.

"She's adorable," Kate said, sitting next to Zora on the couch and quickly replacing her frown with a stilted smile. I sat in the chair.

"We think so," Zora said.

"How are you, Zora? How are things?"

"Things are good. I guess."

Kate turned to me. "Have you seen Talia Ross recently?"

Zora and I made eye contact. "That's random," I said.

"I saw her mom recently. She's living in the same apartment complex as my friend Julie from work."

"We. . . aren't really speaking anymore," I said.

"Oh?"

"Yeah. It's not a big deal."

"That's sad. I always liked her."

"I know you did."

"Maybe you can make up?"

I sighed through my nose. "We went to Aaron's last show," I said. "Everyone loved it." The only way to get Kate let it go was to never speak about it again.

"Oh." She pursed her lips and glanced away.

"What now?" I asked.

"Nothing!"

"It's clearly not nothing."

Kate shrugged. "She's just –"

"He."

"He just refuses to get a full-time job. He's very talented. I just don't know how sustainable this whole music thing is." She looked over at me, frowning. "Both of you are so creative, but that's not really realistic, you know?"

"Well, you're a teacher. That's not like being on Wall Street or anything."

"But your father is a lawyer."

Zora's eyes got wide and she pressed her mouth into a thin line. I rolled my eyes and began, "Kate—"

Kate turned to Zora. "She could call me 'Mom,' you know."

"Oh—"

"Don't do that," I said.

Kate frowned. "Do what?" In that moment, I was thrown back to Talia's, with her asking me if all our problems were in the past. She really didn't know. Neither did Kate.

"Nothing," I said.

***

When you first meet David, you are eight. You spend the summer getting to know him, the father of one of Aaron's friends from first grade. He is in his forties and already balding. Ghostly pale, he often wears sunglasses and a hat, one of the floppy ones with the wide brims meant to protect people not otherwise protected by melanin. He wears T-shirts in the pool to protect his shoulders and back, even though they usually wind up red anyway. Kate befriends his wife and the two of you grew close from the proximity. You are a quiet kid and he lets you be that, no expectations. You two talk about books and the beach and his adult daughter whom you will never meet. She is out of the picture at this point. You laugh at his obvious crush on Kate when he isn't around. Kate thinks it is harmless.

Later, your family sometimes spends holidays at Dave's place, listening to the caroling neighbors and eating latkes by the fire. He never stops flirting with Kate, which she brushes aside like a piece of dust. When you ask her why she doesn't say anything, she shrugs and says, "He doesn't even have sex with his wife." You suppose she pities him.

Dave starts making suggestive comments to you when you in your late teens. Mostly, you ignore them the way your mother did and hope he will stop so you can talk about books again instead of your sex life. You leave his house one Christmas Eve with a hug and feel his hands move down your back, groping when they get low enough. When you tell Kate, she says maybe his hands slipped.

That summer, your family and theirs drive out to Jones Beach for the day. You debate wearing a bikini that trip, wanting to do so without Dave's attention, even though you had only recently started wearing them after years of covering your body. Aaron convinces you to ignore what Dave might say. His daughter is back in the picture then, supposedly having moved closer for the school district. Dave says she moved to be close to him.

Days later, you and him went into the ocean together, just the two of you, like before. You ride the waves and talk about Dave's glory days, when he had long hair and rode a motorcycle. He laments that you didn't know him then, and he looks over at you. "If only I were a few years younger."

When you tell Kate this, she asks you to cut him a break. "He's lonely," she says. You refuse to go back to Dave's house after that. Aaron is no longer close with his son anyway. You let the drift feel natural to everyone else. You don't want resistance for trying to pull away.

***

Of course Marina wanted to go to the beach. I shouldn't have expected anything less of my own daughter. Still, it took me by surprise.

"Are you sure you want to go?" Zora asked me. We were packing for the day. Water bottles. Towels. Sunblock even though none of us really burned.

"I'm sure." I did want to go, really. I was also nervous. Would revisiting the ocean make the feelings flood back? Could that even happen?

Marina ran into the room. "Do you like it?" She spun for us and modeled the bathing suit she'd bought on a trip to the mall with Shauna the previous weekend. It had a strawberry ice cream cone on the top.

"Super cute," Zora said.

Marina smiled. "Yeah."

Zora zipped her bag and looked back at me, her hand out. I took it.

Zora told me once that she hadn't loved the beach until she saw it through my eyes. The endless ocean and the sun's caresses. We walked Marina down to the shallows. A wave rolled over her feet and she jumped back. "Cold!"

"Yeah, it doesn't really warm up until later in the summer," Zora said.

Marina took a tentative step onto the wet sand. "Why?"

Zora shrugged. "That's the way it is."

Another wave rolled onto the sand and Marina stuck her hand out to greet it. Zora looked back at me and smiled. I turned out toward the ocean, so unthreatening in the daytime. It played with my daughter, chasing her in, then running away in some strange game of tag.

I touched Zora's shoulder. "I'm going to sit up on the beach," I said.

"Okay." From further up the shore, I watched Marina play with the water the same way I used to at her age. Would she grow up scared of the water, once she realized what I'd done? I lay back on the towel we'd brought and closed my eyes. What about me? Would I be able to handle it if she wasn't afraid? If she swam out into the sea on warm summer days without thinking about what it could mean to drown?

"Mom!" Marina stood over me now, dripping wet. "I went all the way in!"

I shielded my eyes from the sun and looked up at her. "That's great!"

"Will you come in with me?" she asked. "It's not that cold now."

"You just got used to it."

"Will you come?"

Zora stood at the edge of the water, her skin glowing in the sun. Marina held out her hand for me to take. "Yeah, I'll come."

I followed Marina to the edge of the water. She ran in, shrieked, and then ran back out. "It's cold again!"

"You got out," Zora said. "You have to get used to it again."

Marina pouted but did take another step toward the water, then another. Soon, she was swimming again and laughing. Zora was waist-deep, holding her up when she stopped kicking. "Come on, Mommy!"

I followed Marina's faded footsteps and shuddered at the water's touch. She was right. It was cold.

"You're so slow." Marina rolled her eyes and started

paddling again, ducking under a small wave. I reached them and grabbed onto Zora's shoulder.

"Everything good?" she asked, grabbing my hand in return.

"Yeah." I watched Marina float on the next wave. "It really is."

***

Instead of the standard drinks, Marina and I had made cookies to bring to Kim and Terry's, even though we knew she probably wouldn't eat them. When we got there, Terry took them from Marina and gave her a high-five. "Thanks, Bunny."

"I mixed the chocolate chips in them and everything."

Kim put an arm around Marina. "Top Chef in the house."

Zora put her hands on her hips. "Top Chef over here is going to have to learn how to clean up after herself in the kitchen before she wins any awards."

"Or I could hire maids to do that," Marina said.

Kim burst out laughing. "You're going to have maids?"

"And maybe a butler."

"Hmm. C'mon, Top Chef. You can help Terry finish the salad."

Marina took Terry's hand and headed into the kitchen. Kim sat on the couch and closed her eyes, pressing a hand to her forehead.

I sat next to her. "How are you feeling?"

"Waiting for the aspirin to kick in, and then I'll be great," she said. She lowered her hand and opened her eyes. "You want to help us settle an argument?"

"Always."

Zora sat on the chair, and Kim said, "Terry thinks being a vegetable sounds like a great time. I say not so much."

"Must we?" Terry asked from the kitchen.

"You started it."

"You're completely misrepresenting my words."

Kim waved her hand in his direction. "Whatever. I just said I wouldn't want to be in limbo forever, and he flipped his—" she glanced at Marina, who was tossing salad all over the counter "—you know."

"You know, given the circumstances, I think he's allowed," Zora said.

"Thank you, Zora." Kim rolled her eyes and Terry added, "All I said was that you never know if that person is going to make a miraculous recovery or something."

"But if it were you," Kim asked us, "what would you want?"

Zora thought about it. "Am I in pain?"

"Don't encourage her," Terry said, putting salad on the dining room table.

Kim turned to look at him. "Terry, if I'm in pain, and you're not pulling the plug, I swear when I finally do die, I'm coming back to haunt you."

Terry sat on the arm of the couch next to Kim and kissed her. "You can haunt me," he said. "I wouldn't mind." Kim took his hand.

Marina hopped up on my lap. "Ew, Mommy, they're kissing."

"Sorry, Marina." Terry laughed and pulled Kim up off the couch. "Dinner's ready, anyway."

Marina got down and followed them. "Auntie Kim,

don't you want to live forever?"

"Hon, at this point, I'd like to reach thirty-nine."

"I'd like to live forever," she said, sitting between me and Terry.

Kim sat on Terry's other side and squeezed his shoulder. "Researcher-Uncle Terry will get right on figuring that out," she said.

"Do you think you could be on the other side though?" I asked. "Do you think you could pull the plug if someone you loved was in pain?"

"You people are morbid," Terry said, wrinkling his nose.

Kim looked over at him, then at the table. Her mouth was pressed into a thin line, her eyebrows drawn together in thought.

Terry and Zora didn't get the appeal of thunderstorms, so they stayed inside with Marina while Kim and I watched lightning cut through the sky. Terry told us were crazy, but Kim reminded him that I'm already crazy, so who cares?

"Kim."

"Terry, I'm dying. What's the harm?"

Terry sighed. "You can't use that to win every argument."

Kim shrugged. "I don't see why not." She winked at me over Terry's shoulder.

Later, sitting shielded from the rain by Kim and Terry's front porch in two kitchen chairs Zora and I had dragged outside, Kim said, "I think he's a little afraid of them, honestly. He read a book as a kid where some guy got struck by lightning, and now he hates storms."

"I mean, Zora still won't watch *Beetlejuice* because some friends tried to summon him at a sleepover a million years ago."

Kim laughed along with the thunder. It was a warm night, and although the rain cooled us down a bit, it certainly wasn't cool enough to wear the sweatshirt Kim had on. It was Terry's from Charleston, and it made her look tiny.

Marina ran outside, holding two cookies on a plate. "Uncle Terry says that if you want cookies you have to come inside. So I snuck these."

"I adore you," Kim said, taking a cookie from her.

I laughed and took the plate with the other cookie still on it. Marina ran inside, and Kim put her cookie back on the plate. After a pause, she said, "I'm going to die."

I put the plate by my feet and looked up at her. "Not right now, I hope."

She cracked a smile. "No, not right now. But soon."

"You don't know."

She looked over at me, and our eyes met. "I do."

Thunder roared, and tears threatened to spill out of my eyes. I held them shut for a minute to stem the flow. When I opened them again, Kim was looking up at the sky. "It took me a while, but I'm coming to terms with it," she said. Her own tears slipped down her face. "I'm so tired, Sade."

"You don't know that the chemo won't work," I said.

Kim looked back at me. "Terry doesn't know this yet, so please don't tell. The cancer, it's metastasized. It's. . . in my brain." She took a breath and said, "I'm getting these crazy headaches. . . The odds are almost zero. It's over."

The world dropped out from under me. Brain cancer.

She was talking about brain cancer.

I nodded and gripped my arms with my hands, a false hug. "Well. . . Almost zero still isn't zero."

Kim let out a shaky laugh. "I've been fighting my whole life," she said. "I'm just done with the chemo and whatever treatments. I know when I've lost." We sat in silence for a moment before she said, "You can tell Zora if you want, but just let me tell Terry. Okay?"

"Of course."

"I don't know what happens after, you know, life. But if I can miss you, I know I will."

I took her hand, and she rested my head on her shoulder. "I'll miss you too," I said. We sat there for half an hour, at least. Lightning flashed though the sky, illuminating the clouds.

THE SIXTH LETTER: FROM THE FIRST

Dear Kate,

I don't know where to start with this letter. It is you I have the most history with—thirty-five years' worth of fighting and loving and crying, both to you and because of you. That is why I saved this letter for last, hoping inspiration would strike in the words I wrote to Talia or Krishna or Avery. I suppose though that letters chose where to start, though, if you write them the way they're supposed to be written. This one starts with your name.

You asked me once to call you "Mom." I was twenty, and I had already been calling you "Kate" for ten or so years. It was soon after your divorce to my and Aaron's father. He left you with no income and mounting debt and phone calls from the banks. When you consulted a lawyer, she told you to change your phone number. You did, but they still called. I learned this too early, in your room in the old house in Ditmas Park. You cried to me, and I handed you tissues on your bed.

A friend commented to me just a few years ago that I seemed like your mother, not your daughter. She meant it as a joke, after I told her about us coming back from California. It was right before Zora and I were to start fostering Marina, and we decided to take one last trip together before motherhood rendered me home-bound for a time. Or rather, I had a conference in San Francisco, and you decided that you wanted to come along. Your exact words, in fact, were "Maybe I'll come."

"Do you mean, 'Can I come?'" I asked.

You thought about it, as though you hadn't considered that I might want to go on a work trip without my mother. In the end, you came anyway, upgrading what would have been an AirBnB to a Marriott and paying for meals you shouldn't have splurged on. I sound ungrateful, and maybe I am. Honestly, I'm torn between thankful and fearful when I think of you with money. You're always willing to give, and I love that about you, but I also know that your status as a single mother and elementary school teacher haven't quite squashed the habits from your childhood of wealth.

The comment from a friend came when I mentioned the flights. You, anxious, fidgeting, and asking me if I thought we would make our connecting flight. Me, exasperated but not wanting to appear as though I didn't want you there with me, handing you my phone to play games on the way down. The friend compared you to her own daughter, who has trouble sitting through long car rides without her mother's iPad.

It's clear to me that the women in our family have never been prepared to be mothers. Not my great-grandmother who spent my grandmother's childhood reeling from the losses of the Holocaust. Not my grandmother, your mother, who wanted more than anything to travel. Her dreams came to a halt as an eighteen-year-old girl when she met your father in New York, a handsome man five years her senior with whom she fell in love. She got married young and had you and your sister, born to a mother who would always regret her title.

But you had always wanted children, even if you weren't prepared to raise them on your own. You married my father, a lawyer with anger-management problems and a history of abuse and alcoholism, and even when you were together, you were essentially a single mom. Did Aaron ever tell you how much he wanted our father's blue eyes, even though he was adopted? He used to complain about his, too brown. I told him he would have looked dumb with blue eyes.

You didn't know what to do with me. I wouldn't leave the house unless I could only wear one shoe, something therapists was later theorized was OCD-related, though they weren't sure how. When Aaron finally came home, I bit him. And then Aaron turned out to be even more of a terror than I had been. If I wouldn't let him sit in my chair, he would punch and bite me until I relented. When we adopted a cat, a brown and white tabby with particularly fluffy ears and a stub of a tail, Aaron would sit on her and pull her ears. Once, he went on a rampage, kicking and hitting me until you locked me in your bedroom with you. Aaron pounded on the door outside, surprisingly thunderous bangs for such small fists, until he exhausted himself and retreated to his room down the hall. No one thought until later that he had been imitating our father.

When Aaron and I get together, we are the ultimate team. For so long I hated the way he followed me around, but he was also my consistent playmate and best friend. I was six or seven when we decided I would cut his hair. You found us with Aaron's hair on the floor in pieces and interrupted my work-in-progress. I remember how he looked like a balding man stuck in a child's body.

Once, Aaron and I were playing frisbee in the house when I missed Aaron—I have never and will never play a sport outside of high school gym—and hit the big window in the living room instead. It shattered, cracks coming together like a spider web. When you heard the noise and found us, you sighed. "Well, we needed a new window anyway," you said. We never spoke about it after that.

You've complained more than once that Aaron and I gang up on you when we're together, that we're unfair. You have asked me if I'm Aaron's lawyer, but never asked me why I feel like I need to be. Do you remember when Aaron was thinking about coming back north after school? It was his senior year at Charlotte, and he was looking to be in Massachusetts or New Jersey, mostly for the seasons. You were still on his case for getting a degree in music over business. I reminded you that just because you regretted not majoring in business didn't mean Aaron would too. You didn't like that.

Still, you've singled me out in ways that you would never do to Aaron. When you tell me you hate my hair, or that you love my hair but it could look "so much better" shorter, or that you love this haircut because the other one looked terrible. Or else, you beg me to wax my eyebrows even when I say I like the way they look. Aaron tried to talk to you about that, I know. Mostly now you talk about my body when he's not around.

Food too, is something we touch on often in ways that remind me of how I once viewed my body as the enemy. You tell me I'm too thin, and then talk about how fat you look in a photo. You comment on how well I've eaten, and then go to the gym after "eating too much." You aren't the reason my relationship with my body grew so tumultuous, but you didn't help, either. When I tell you this, you scoff and tell me I should go back to therapy. Aaron has asked you to stop talking about food too, but you haven't listened.

It's a pattern, I think, for you. To view women as something that need to be fixed, or else a threat. You and your sister were close, once, until you weren't. You never met her kids, until last year, when her son reached out to you. You told me that you didn't want to meet her daughter, afraid that, in your words, she would be a bitch. I asked you why you didn't think that about your nephew, and you said you didn't know. I can't help but wonder how different our relationship would be if I were a man, or how that will change your relationship with my daughter.

The first time you saw her, Marina was three-years-old. Zora and I had officially adopted her a week earlier with promises to call her birth mom—something you hardily disapproved of—and too-wide smiles that promised to split our faces. For the year and a half leading up to the adoption, when Zora and I were foster parents, you constantly asked me if I was sure I wanted to be a mother, even though I'd taken every step to ensure that, this time, a woman in our family would be prepared for what came after. When we brought her home for forever, I asked if you wanted to meet her, and you did. Then you asked me again if I knew what I was doing, and if the adoption really was permanent.

After thirty years of knowing you, of hating you, of loving you, I should have been prepared, an invisible shield at the ready to repel your words. But I wasn't, and they nearly knocked me down with their force. Nearly. My daughter is six now, and you hadn't seen her in three years before I decided Marina could handle it, and that I could too. You kept asking, but I keep making excuses. I wasn't sure I could handle another battle with your insecurities about my own being.

Not speaking with you, not letting you be a part of my daughter's life, those were not decisions I made lightly. I spent nights crying about what I'd done, but honestly, I don't regret it. Your words already planted seeds of doubt in my own mind. You made me feel small, less than human. Even now that we are speaking again, I try to maintain some distance for my own wellbeing.

I told Aaron about my therapist's assignment, to write these letters. He asked me if I would write one to you. The funny thing is, I think this letter would come as a surprise to you. I don't know that you think of us as complicated, or that you see any antagonism as mutual. I see myself more clearly now than I have, my physical being as well as just me. But when I try to picture myself through your eyes, I see someone unfit to be Marina's mother, to be Zora's wife, to be your daughter. These are the things I need to overcome to feel at home in my skin.

Kate, I love you. I have never not. I need you to know

that, even if parts of this letter will hurt, even if I can picture you reading this letter in my mind, with your eyebrows scrunched together in confusion and your mouth trembling in frustration. It would be too much, and I know that. Part of me still wants to protect you from that, to be your mother, as I've already been told I am in an offhand comment from a friend. Our relationship is complicated—but it's my most important, and that matters.

All my love,
Sadie

<u>GONE</u>

"Hit me."

Terry slapped another card down on the table and Kim grinned, laying hers out. "Twenty-one, bitches!"

"I think this game is rigged," Zora said, throwing her sixteen down and crossing her arms. We were at Kim and Terry's house, and Terry had made us some virgin something with passion fruit and oranges, since two of us weren't drinking anymore. He'd decorated them with pineapple wedges on the sides.

"It's just good karma," Kim said. "I might be dead tomorrow."

"You know she's going to keep saying that for weeks," Terry said, laughing. Kim grinned up at him and leaned in for a kiss.

"I think we need a dealer that isn't married to Kim," Zora said. I laughed.

"Fine. Sorest loser deals," Kim said, passing the cards

to Zora. Zora made a face, but she was laughing too.

"Just you wait," she said, and dealt the cards. Kim won that round with a twenty.

"What was it you said again?" Kim asked, smirking. Zora scowled and lay down her twenty-four. Kim stood. "Play this next round without me. Maybe you'll actually win."

Zora grew suddenly serious. "You okay?"

"Yeah, I'll be right back." Zora dealt the cards.

I won that game with nineteen and glanced at Zora, apologetic. "Next one?"

"Mmhmm." She stopped, sniffed the air. "Terry, is your wife smoking pot?"

The air had become infused with the sweet scent of plants. Terry inhaled, then sighed. "It's medical," he said. "It means she's in pain."

"Should we check on her?" I asked.

Terry opened his mouth to answer when Kim came back into the room and sat down between Zora and Terry. "Reprieve over," she told Zora.

Zora gathered the cards and began to shuffle them. "Are you sure you're okay?"

"Just deal," Kim said. She caught me looking at her hands on the cards as Zora passed them over, trembling slightly. We locked eyes, hers rimmed with dark circles, and she hid her hands under the table.

We played until Zora won just one game (it took a long time, even when she was dealing the cards) and got home just before midnight. Zora's mom, Angel, greeted us at the door.

"Thanks for watching her, Mami," Zora said, putting her bag down on the table.

"Are you kidding? I'd watch Marina all the time if I could."

"We'll see you soon?" I asked. Truth be told, Angel hadn't been too keen on becoming a grandparent, especially since she'd had Zora so young. Now that it had happened, she couldn't get enough.

Angel gripped my hand. "Of course."

"Can I drive you home?" Zora asked.

She shook her head. "I'm not far."

"I know but –"

"It's fine."

"It's late."

"I promise, I can navigate one train."

"Okay, okay," Zora said. Angel hugged us both, grabbed her purse, and left.

Zora sat on the couch, and I followed her. "You don't need to worry about her," I said. "She's a big girl."

Zora laughed. "I know, I know."

"Do you think Kim was right?"

"What? About her being the superior Black Jack player? Fuck that."

"You know what I mean. About dying. . . soon." Dying *tomorrow* just seemed a bit too real for me to say out loud.

Zora sat up straighter and took my hand. "Honestly, Sadie, I don't know. She looked okay tonight. But Terry said she was in pain. I just don't know."

I nodded. Zora scooted closer to me and put her arm around my shoulders. She kissed me, and I let myself forget.

This is what happened later, based on what Terry told us. Kim woke up at some ungodly hour of the night with a nosebleed, a bad one. Terry heard her get up and followed her to the bathroom down the hall. They stayed there for a while, with Kim bent over the sink and Terry helping her clean up what must have looked like a crime scene. She made several inappropriate jokes about death, I'm sure. Several times, she nearly fell asleep like that, standing hunched over and covered in her own blood. Hours after they'd gone back to bed, she woke up again with debilitating vertigo and a fever of 102. That's when Terry took her to the hospital.

The cramps wake you up. For a moment, you think you are a teenager again with pre-birth control period pains, until you feel the king-sized sheets under you and hear your wife breathing softly beside you. You are not a teenager with a bad menstrual cycle. You are thirty-four, and you are pregnant.

You whisper your wife's name once, then again. She startles out of her sleep and flicks the lights on. When you throw back the blanket, you see the blood.

Zora shoots up and grabs the bag you'd packed for this moment. She helps you to your feet. You sway, and she grabs your arm. "Can you make it?"

In truth, you don't know, but you say you can. You throw on a pair of unbloodied underwear and a dress you got from some maternity section somewhere. It isn't important. You sit in the passenger's side on the way to the hospital and try to minimize the pain in your body. You sit cross-legged, then crouched, then with your feet up on the dashboard. None of it helps.

Kim refused to call an ambulance, he said. The room

spun out from under her as she attempted to sit and she threw up into a trashcan, Terry holding her up. She struggled to get out of bed, shivering in a thin sweater. Terry scooped her up and took her out to the car. He piled her high with blankets for the five-minute drive and took off. He kept talking to keep her conscious, probably something like, "How are you doing, baby?" or "You're going to be fine. You're going to be okay," or "I love you. So much." Kim wouldn't have spoken much at all.

Terry called me in hysterics around noon. "Please come," he whispered.

"I'm on my way," I said, grabbing my bag. "Do you want me to stay on the line?"

"No. I'll be in Kim's room," he said.

"Okay, ETA an hour and a half."

I called Aaron and asked him to pick up Marina and left a message for Zora telling her where I'd be. I broke the speed limit all the way to General and made it in an hour. A nurse found me in the hallway and brought me to Kim.

You forget for long periods of time how to breathe. In, then out, then in, then in—no, then out, then in. You focus on that for a while, until another contraction punches through you. You hear yourself screaming, but it's as though you hear it from a distance, from someone else. All you are is the blood, the contractions, the pain.

The monitors beeped and blinked numbers at me that I didn't understand. I sat in a chair next to Terry and saw with a rush of relief that Kim was awake. "How bad is it?"

Kim exhaled slowly and winced. Her lips were chapped and her eyes were hazy with illness and drugs. Her IV was connected to her right hand, which probably meant they couldn't find a vein in her arms. "Everything hurts," she whispered. "My whole body hurts." She shivered and Terry stroked her hair.

He looked up at me, his eyes wet and puffy. He still wore pajama pants. "Thank you so much for coming."

"Zora called me back while I was on my way here. She'll come as soon as she can."

Kim shifted on the bed and moaned quietly. "She has to come quick," she said.

Terry lifted squeezed her hand. "Baby, just rest."

Did you pass out just now? You're not sure. Next to you, your wife is telling you to hold on. In the intermittent moments between debilitating waves of agony, you feel. You feel the blood beneath your legs, sticky and still wet. You feel the paper-thin hospital gown over your stretched-out stomach. You feel Zora's hand in yours, the ring that matches the one you wear on your left hand, the ones you exchanged when you exchanged vows and promised to be with each other in sickness and in health. Would Zora have made that promise if she'd known this was coming? Would you have?

Your other senses overwhelm you all of a sudden. They were gone, and now they're the only thing that's here. The taste of bile on your tongue. The smell of antiseptic and sweat. The sound of a baby crying in the distance. Asher's sound.

Zora ran into the hospital room still in her lab coat. She sat next to me, reached out to put a hand on Kim's arm. Terry was sitting on the bed with Kim now, his arms around her shoulders. "Hey, girl," Zora said.

Kim glanced in her direction with glassy eyes. "I told you," she mumbled. "Blackjack. Good karma."

"Nah, you're just better than me."

Kim exhaled what might have been a laugh or a groan. It was too quiet to tell. "You're just saying that because I'm dying." None of us said anything to that. She shivered again and leaned into Terry. "I'm scared."

"You'll be okay," Terry said. His voice shook and he held her tighter. "I'm not leaving."

"I know." Kim closed her eyes. She fell asleep within a minute.

Zora and I stayed with Terry until the end of visiting hours in the hopes that Kim would wake up again. She did, one more time. A sharp intake of breath. We all looked over and saw Kim squeeze her eyes shut tighter.

"Kim? Kim, what's wrong?"

"Can you. . . Fuck. . ." She gasped and grabbed her head with one hand, gripped Terry's hand tight with the other. I ran out of the room to the nearest nurses, standing at the end of the hall. "My friend in room 202, Kim Salazar, is there anything else you can give her?"

One of them shook his head. "No, I'm sorry. She's at her limit."

"What happens when you go over the limit?"

The two nurses glanced at each other and the other one said, "She could die."

I glanced back at the room, then looked the second nurse in the eye. "That doesn't matter." The nurses looked at each other again, and then back at me. The second one went to give her morphine.

In a state somewhere between semi-consciousness and death, you see everything. You see yourself sledding down a hill with Aaron and your cousins, Avery and Johanna. You and Aaron are on one sled, Avery and Johanna on the other. You all race down the hill until you crash into a snowbank piled high at the foot of it, and then you run to the top to do it again.

You see Kate crying in the kitchen of the house you grew up in. It is the house she would lose, and she and you and Aaron would move in with your grandparents for all of middle school and early high school. Several times, your grandmother would threaten to kick you all out. At least twice, you stayed with a friend, though you didn't know if it was because your grandmother had gotten her way or because Kate couldn't take it anymore.

Just before we left, Terry turned to us. "She's going to die," he said. In spite of his long conversation with Zora and the many doctor appointments he'd taken Kim to over the last couple of months—in spite of him being in medicine himself, even—it was like he had just realized it.

Zora walked back over to him and put a hand on his shoulder. "Yes," she said.

Kim was right about besting us all at card games, but she was wrong too. She didn't die that day. She made it another five. The day after she'd been admitted we came again, but Kim mostly slept.

"It was really bad," Terry told us over her failing body. "She woke up last night screaming. . ."

"Hang in there, Terry," Zora said. She squeezed his hand in hers. He hung his head.

My eyes found the bags under his. "Terry, when's the

last time you ate something?"

He frowned. "Ate something?"

"Yeah. You know, food."

"I'm not hungry."

"I know," I said. "You still need to eat." I got up and stood at his side, gently taking his arm. "C'mon."

He looked over at Zora, like she would protest on his behalf. Instead, she said, "I'll sit with her."

He let me lead him to the cafeteria, where I ordered him a sandwich and a coffee. We sat down at a sticky cafeteria sable, and Terry picked at the edge of the coffee cup.

"You have to eat," I said.

"Yeah." He made no move to do so. Out of nowhere, he put his head in his hands and began to cry. I put my arms around him, holding him like I would hold Marina. In between sobs, he apologized. "I'm sorry," he said.

"Shh." I held him tighter and let him cry.

You see yourself and your brother visiting your father as young teens. He is hesitant around you then, somewhat hopeful that if he behaves himself, you will stay. Some cracks are just too big to be mended, though. When you stay in the psych hospital the first time, he asks Kate if he can come see you, and Kate leaves it to you. You say no. You see him one more time, at Aaron's Bar Mitzvah. He corners you when your friends are on the dance floor, and asks you, begs you, to visit him. You say nothing.

You see yourself meeting Zora at a party some friends dragged you to in grad school. She is beautiful, wearing her hair in the same braids she would wear later, to your wedding. A friend notices you staring and introduces you. When Zora smiles, you forget why you didn't want to come to the party after all.

Kim woke up once, toward the end of our visit. She shifted in the bed, and Terry sat up straighter, leaning toward her. "Hey, baby."

She cracked her eyes open, and they fell on me and Zora. She sighed. "Don't you have anything better to do than watch me die?"

"Nope," I told her. "This is the best we can do."

Kim closed her eyes again. She reached for Terry, and he took her hand. "My head is pounding."

"They said they can't give you any more drugs," Terry said, eyeing the door.

"Fuck them," she mumbled.

Zora turned toward the door, too. "I'll ask," she said, and she left the room.

"Are you dizzy?" Terry asked.

"Hmm." Kim frowned. "A little. Not so bad."

"How's the rest of the pain?"

"Ugh."

Terry stroked her hair. Several strands fell onto the pillow. "Is there anything I can do for you?"

Kim took a breath and gave him a small smile. "No. Just stay with me."

You see yourself at your wedding, dizzy with nerves. Both of you wear white dresses and, later, matching gold bands on your fingers. You see yourself meeting your daughter for the first time and holding her tiny two-year-old hand in yours. You see taking her to the beach and reading to her at night. You see the appointments leading up to pregnancy, and then your pregnant belly, expanded to contain another someone to love.

Later, when you leave without him, when are in the psych hospital, you will see his face, so small, so much like yours it hurts. You will see Zora, broken, and Marina, asking you why her little brother died. You will feel all of it, and you will feel none of it.

After two days of fluctuating fever and not enough morphine, Kim fell into a coma. Terry was almost relieved. We came on day four, and this time Zora took Terry downstairs to get coffee and something to eat while I stayed with Kim. I glanced up at the machines, giving me numbers I still couldn't decipher—Zora would have been able explain them—but that I knew meant Kim wasn't going to make it this time. I leaned in close and whispered, "I don't know if you can hear me. I'm just going to miss you. You know that already, but I just wanted to make sure. . ."

Breathe in, breathe out.

"I wrote you a letter," I told her. "Is that okay? Most of them I'll never send, but I would have let you read yours. I *will* let you read yours, if you make it out of this. It doesn't say anything you don't know. I just wanted to tell you how much I love you. Because I do. A lot." I twisted her fingers in mine and squeezed. I heard Zora and Terry walking up the hall, then, and wiped my eyes.

Zora is next to you the whole time. When you wake, so does she, quickly reminding you that you're safe, in the hospital, not alone. "I'm here," she says, reaching out for you. You whisper Asher's name. Zora bursts into tears.

"I'm sorry," she says. "I'm so sorry." This is how you learn your son is dead.

"Sadie?" I'd just closed my laptop and turned to see Zora in the doorway of our bedroom. Her breathing was in quick gasps. She had just come from the hospital.

"What? What happened?"

"Kim—Oh God—"

I went to her and took her in my arms. Zora grabbed onto me, and we both cried. She managed to tell me that Kim's brother and her grandparents made it out, and some friends from when she wasn't sick. Her parents couldn't make it in time from the Philippines, but they FaceTimed through her brother before the coma took her away. When Kim died, it was just Zora, Terry, and a nurse. I don't remember going to sleep that night, but I must have, because I woke up, tears still on my pillow.

WHAT COMES NEXT

I nearly canceled on Rosa that week, but Zora asked me to go. "I don't want to leave you here alone again," she said. I'd left our room only a handful of times over the three days between Kim's death and therapy with Rosa. To get Marina from school. A few times to use the bathroom. Twice to eat, and only then because Zora made me.

"Please," she said. "I know. I'm hurting too."

Another beat, and I nodded. Zora exhaled and kissed me on the cheek.

Rosa didn't comment on my appearance, even though I hadn't showered in three days and had barely run my fingers through my hair on the subway to make it at least somewhat presentable. She wore a pantsuit. I wore jean shorts and an old tank top. I sat down across from her and said, "Kim died. Three days ago."

"I'm so sorry," Rosa said. "She meant a lot to you."

I shrugged. "I didn't want to come here. Zora asked me

to and she was right, I think. I knew I was, I mean, I don't know what. . ." I shook my head and started over. "I feel like I did after Asher. . ." A tear slipped down my cheek and I slapped it away.

"You feel the same way you did after your son died," Rosa said.

I nodded. "It just hurts," I said. "My heart hurts."

"I'm really glad you came today," Rosa said. "I didn't know Kim, but I can't imagine she'd want you to sit in your room and go back to that dark place over her."

"No. She wouldn't." I sighed and sat back on the couch. "I just don't know how to do this."

"Do what?"

"Not. . . have a fucking breakdown," I said. "I don't know how to grieve like a normal person. And I don't want to have a breakdown. Ugh!" I stood and started pacing back and forth. "Kim was good. She was a good fucking person. And this is just shit. It's all shit. She didn't want to die. Do you know what she said to her husband when I was at the hospital? She said she was scared. She wasn't ready. There are so many people like me who just want to end it and how is it that someone like Kim who's so good and has so much to offer the world and who wasn't ready to die is just gone?" I was crying again, but I didn't care. "I just want to understand it. Everything is so fucking mixed up in my head and I know that none of it really matters be-cause we all die anyway but I know that and I still just can't—" I sat back on the couch, my chest heaving. I felt Rosa next to me, putting her arm around me. In, then out, then in, then in—no, then out, then in. . .

When I'd somewhat remembered how to breathe, Rosa said, "All of this that you're feeling? It's so normal.

It's not fair. Nothing about this is fair. And it sucks that you have to deal with this, especially so soon after your son."

I sat back, looking at Rosa. She had tears in her eyes.

"How do I do it, though?" I asked.

Rosa sighed. "You just do."

Zora came home late that night, after a double shift. She startled when she realized I was still up, sitting in the living room with the TV on low.

"Hey." She came over and sat next to me. "How was it with Rosa?"

"It was good," I said. "I needed it."

"That's good."

I turned to her. "I need you to help me," I said. "I don't really know how to do the whole healthy grieving thing and I'm not sure I can. But I have to try. For you and Marina."

Zora nodded. "And for you."

"And for me."

Zora smiled, put a hand on my face. I leaned into it. "Of course I'll help you."

"I'm not easy. I know that."

"I knew that when I married you," she said. I laughed and she said, "Really. I love you. All of you. And I hate what the depression does to you, and how it makes you feel. But that doesn't mean I don't love depressed you."

I nodded and sat closer to her, my head on her shoulder. "I know that too."

***

Not once during the ceremony did Zora let go of my hand, and I clung to it like I would float away if she let go. Kim was a very, very lapsed Catholic, but her parents insisted on a priest, a mass, all that. Terry didn't mind. Terry didn't have very many opinions, actually, although he drew the line at forty days of prayer at his house.

After, we moved to stand by him in the cemetery. He trembled the whole time, trying to sob as silently as possible. He was the only one wearing long sleeves in the summer heat. Zora kept a hand on his arm. We watched the coffin descend into the ground. With a single thought—Kim is in there—the floodgates opened, and tears poured down my face. I glanced over at Zora, and she squeezed my hand. She was crying too.

The three of us sat among the church pews for at least an hour after everyone else had left. Several times, friends and family came over to offer Terry their condolences, and we accepted them on his behalf. He didn't speak almost that whole time, until the last of the mourners—Kim's brother, her parents, her grandparents—left. He said, "I don't want to go home."

"We'll go with you," I said, and Zora nodded.

"Marina—"

"She's with Shauna," Zora said.

Terry took a deep breath and dissolved into tears again. He buried his head in his hands and howled.

What is it with tragedy that makes people want to bring the victims soup? Their fridge was full of it. I closed the door and sighed. None of us were very hungry anyway. Instead, I let the water on the stove boil and poured us tea.

Terry sighed as I handed him a mug, a silent 'Thank

you.' I'd almost used Kim's #1 Karate Teacher mug, until I realized what it was. The three of us sat on the couch together, Terry in the middle.

I understood why Terry hadn't wanted to be here. The whole place recalled Kim's life. The photos of the two of them on the walls. The yellow blanket folded on the couch. The broken dining room chair she'd fixed with a hot glue gun and reassembled two summers ago. Terry seemed to think along these lines, at least. His eyes jumped from one object to the next, memories leaping out of each.

"I never went to Asher's grave." Zora and Terry both turned to look at me. I shrugged and said, "Just. . . thinking."

"We'll go," Zora said. "We can go whenever you want."

"Yeah."

None of us said anything for a while, and then Terry set his mug on the table. "I keep playing back those last few days. She just looked. . . so sick." He wiped his eyes on his sleeve. "She was in so much pain."

Zora rubbed the back of her neck. "She's not anymore."

"I would have taken it from her if I could. I would have switched places."

"We know," I said. "She knew that too."

"I keep thinking she's going to be there. When I wake up in the morning. Just turning the corner, I keep expecting to see her." His voice shook, and he covered his face with his hands.

"I know," I said, my own voice unsteady. I put my mug on the table, next to Terry's. "I know. It'll take time."

He looked back at me with bloodshot eyes. "How much time?"

I glanced over at Zora, then back at Terry. "I don't know."

***

My hand grabbed at the empty space next to me when I woke up, and I glanced at the clock. It was four in the morning. Still too early for Zora to be up for work.

I pulled a thin sheet around my bare shoulders and tread quietly past Marina's room. I found Zora in the kitchen, leaning against the island counter with her forehead resting on the palm of her hands. She looked up as I got closer. "Hey."

"Couldn't sleep?"

Zora shook her head. "I didn't mean to wake you."

"You didn't." She sighed and I said, "Do you want to talk about it?"

"I just keep. . . seeing her." She put her palms against her forehead again and said, "I keep seeing her dying." Deep breath. "I did something bad, Sadie."

My heart leapt into my mouth. "What do you mean?"

Zora hesitated. "She was in so much pain." Breathe in, breathe out.

"Zora?"

"You're going to hate me."

"I could never hate you."

Zora began pacing. "You don't know. You don't know what I did."

I reached out and grabbed her arm. She jumped a little at the contact. "Zora. I love you. Whatever it is."

She shuddered, and then collapsed to the floor, sobbing. I knelt down next to her and wrapped her in the

150

sheet I wore. "Hey, it's okay. I love you. You're okay."

We stayed like that for a while, until Zora caught her breath and said, "I killed her, Sadie." I didn't say anything, just let her keep talking. "She wasn't going to get better. It wasn't going away, and then it was in her brain. . ."

A distant conversation came back to me. Rodney, what had he said about morphine? *You can die from too much of that shit. Your heart stops and you just don't wake up.* I took a breath. "Does Terry know?"

Zora shook her head against my chest. "He wouldn't have done it. He would hate me. Oh, God, Sadie."

"Hey, it's okay." I gripped her tighter.

"I killed her."

"It's okay." She sobbed harder, and I ran my fingers through her hair. "You're okay," I said. "We're going to get through this."

THE SEVENTH LETTER: LIGHTS

Dear Kim,

I didn't like you when we first met. Zora and I had been married for a year and she came home all excited one day. She'd made a friend at work, finally, and he wanted us to come over for dinner with him and his then-fiancée. You were living in Manhattan, and we took the train up to the East Side. You were sarcastic and aloof and I couldn't quite figure you out. It wasn't until later I realized I wasn't used to your honesty. It was brutal at first, but you ended up helping me through a lot by being you.

Until I met you, I never used to talk about depression, anxiety, OCD. I'd nervously relayed some of my past to Zora, and a few of my closest friends knew, but you talked about your body and your past pain so freely it made me rethink why I hadn't. I think the second time I met you,

you mentioned having had cancer. I must have said something like, "What?" because you said,

"Yeah, leukemia. The only thing more fun was the depression." Terry suppressed a laugh at my reaction. I stared at you, shell shocked. It had never even occurred to me what it might sound like to talk about being sick. From you, it sounded so normal.

In one of the most crowded and lonely cities on earth, you and Terry were a dream come true. You were there for us when we went through fostering Marina, and you sat behind us at the courthouse when she officially became ours. I actually cried when you moved to New Jersey, even though we saw you still at least once a month. Your visits in the psych hospital reminded me that I would be okay, that living wasn't the worst thing. And you were there for me after, even when you got so sick yourself. I'd like to think you needed me too, but I know that I wouldn't have made it through without you. I don't know how I'll make it through without you now.

I wrote a rough draft of this letter before you died, when Terry called and told us you'd fallen into a coma. I came back to it later (now). I don't feel differently about you at all, but losing you was a pain so deep I could only return to words. It's physical, when you lose someone. Depression is odd because it both numbs the pain and amplifies it until it becomes unbearable, until you want to dive into the Atlantic and never come out. You and I had talked about this before. You'd never known what it had been like to want to die, but after your second battle with leukemia, depression had aquatinted itself with you in a different way. For a while, you forgot what it was like to be happy. I've known that feeling. It's terrifying.

Some of my favorite memories of you are just us talking. Before you moved and Terry and Zora worked at the same hospital, we ditched them one night at some fancy doctor gala and brought drinks into the bathroom lounge. We played truth or dare. You asked me what my biggest fear was.

"Zora realizing she doesn't love me," I said.

You laughed at me. "Well that's dumb," you said.

"Excuse me?"

"She's obviously in love with you."

I explained to you that I had a long history of depression and anxiety and all these things weighing down on me, and that Zora had never really seen them, not like they could be. She wouldn't love me if she knew. You looked at me and said, "You're not very smart, are you?" I still can't believe that made me feel better.

You were right about a lot of things. You were right when you told me once, visiting me in the hospital, that I would get through it. I did. I'm struggling to stay on this side, but I did. You were right that depressed is still sick, and that I had to stop blaming myself for being that way. I still struggle with that sometimes, but I'm working on it. You were wrong though about something too, though. Getting well isn't about dumb luck, even with the drugs. I've had to be strong to do what I do, and you had to be strong too. There are plenty of people who don't make it through, even though they were perhaps braver than I've ever been. You were one of them. I suppose that was part of your point. But if you can't get well even with bravery, you definitely can't get well without it.

Maybe. Maybe I have to think that so that I can continue to be brave. I don't know all the answers. I guess I'm still trying to figure it out.

Sometimes I used to forget you were human. You seemed so far above the rest of us, but you weren't invincible. I somehow felt both honored and frightened when you opened up to me about your own fears. I feel guilty about that now, and I promise I always wanted to be there for you, regardless. You were just everything I wanted to be. Fearless in the face of illness. Unapologetic about what that meant.

Do you remember apologizing to me in the park for taking a break when we were walking around the water? It was a small moment, something nearly insignificant, and something I'd done so many times. But it felt strange to be on the other side, reassuring you that you didn't have to apologize for something you couldn't control. When you told Terry you were scared after you went into the hospital for the last time, my heart broke. You had the right to be scared, even if you had accepted what was coming. A small, selfish part of me expected you not to be.

Seeing Terry after you died scared me. He's so lost and so broken. Zora has done this before, helping someone she loved through their pain even when she was hurting, too. We'll have to do this for Terry. Know that we love him, and we'll keep loving him. He won't be alone, just like you wouldn't have left Zora alone if something had happened to me. He's kind of stuck with us.

Little things are harder than I think they'd be, like bringing Marina to a friend's and seeing the younger brother at the door in a karate belt. It was white, which you taught me means he's just starting out. Other things are less so. I thought that telling Marina that you had died would kill me, and we all cried, of course, but I'm still standing.

None of us will ever meet someone like you again. That honestly sucks, but I think I knew when we became friends that there would never be another you. You were special. You still are. Wherever you are, I hope you're not in pain anymore. I hope you're happy. You deserve it.

With love,

Sadie

BEGIN AGAIN

Terry took a few weeks of work after Kim died, which meant he spent a lot of time coming into Brooklyn, trying to get out of the house that so painfully recalled his life with her. Once, we talked about the cost of the funeral, and I realized why Kim hadn't wanted to take an ambulance to the hospital in the end.

He cried a lot at first, and then less. He debated moving back to Charleston to be with family but didn't want to move away from the support he had here and from where he'd been with Kim. Some days he sat almost catatonic, and I made him tea and forced him to eat something. Some days, he talked about her non-stop.

"She had to leave college for a while," he said once. "After the cancer came back a second time. She was twenty. When she went back, she'd started working at Sammy's part-time and my friends and I went one night. We were both twenty-seven. I was the DD, so I sat at the bar and got ready to order a virgin something or other. Probably a Mai Tai. And then I saw her. I mean, I never believed in love at first sight, but she was just so ... You know?"

I nodded. We were sitting at the kitchen table in my apartment. Zora was at work, Marina with Shauna for the day. He continued, "I ordered my drink and she laughed at me. She actually laughed. She said something like, 'You don't want that one. You want this.' And she made me a virgin hurricane instead. I never ordered anything else after that. She taught me how to make it, later."

"I know," I said. I'd had it.

Terry blinked and looked over at me, seeming to remember that he was talking to someone, then kept going. "I went back to the bar a few more times with my friends and offered to DD more than I probably would have otherwise. Sometimes she wasn't there, but I kept going back just so I could talk to her when she was. Finally, she was like, 'So when are you going to ask me out?'"

"That sounds like Kim," I said.

"We dated for a long time. She didn't know if she wanted to get married. A lot of that was because she didn't want someone else to deal with the cancer if it ever came back. When she said yes. . . I don't know how I ever convinced her."

"She loved you," I said. "She wanted to marry you."

"I'm so lost without her, Sadie. What do I have to live for now?"

So many people would tell him to live on for Kim. I knew that. I didn't want to tell him that. At some point, he'd have to move on. Not yet, but some day. And he had us to live for, but I knew I'd had so many people I loved before Asher died, and I'd still gone off the deep end, literally. "You live for you," I said.

I heard a knock on the door then, squeezed Terry's hand, and got up to answer it. Marina ran in past Shauna and hugged me around the legs. "Hi, Mommy!"

"Hi, Bunny," I laughed. I looked up at Shauna. "Did you have a nice time?"

"We did. We went to Prospect."

"Yeah. Mama Shauna took me to get ice cream too." She spotted Terry at the table and squealed. "Uncle Terry!"

"Hey, Bunny." He scooped my giggling daughter up in his arms and smiled for the first time in weeks.

***

I'd forgotten the wraps again, but it turns out you can get them at the boxing gym. I picked up my gloves and got ready to leave the locker room when a woman with thick blonde hair in a pink sports bra approached me. "You're Kim's friend, aren't you?"

She looked vaguely familiar? "Oh. Yes."

"I saw you here with her once," the woman said. "I'm Claudia."

Oh, right. From the bathroom. "Sadie." We shook hands.

"How is Kim, by the way? I heard she was sick and I haven't seen her in a while."

My stomach lurched. "She. . . died."

"Oh."

"A few weeks ago."

"I'm so sorry. I didn't know."

Obviously. "Yeah, I don't really box. I just thought, I

mean, she always said it was good for you and—" I took a breath, then another.

"It is. It builds some great muscle."

"Mostly she was talking about endorphins, I think." I looked the woman in the eye. "I have depression. I was hospitalized this past year, and I thought I'd give it a shot."

"Oh." Claudia took a step back and said, "Well, good luck." She turned around and scurried away.

I sat back down on the bench and exhaled. Feelings bumped up against each other in my brain. Embarrassment. Exhilaration. Kim's voice in the back of my mind asked me who cared, anyway, and suddenly the embarrassment vanished, just like that.

***

I didn't expect her, but Kate had come, and she was standing at my door. "What are you doing here?"

"You weren't answering my phone calls," she said.

Deep breath. "It's been. . . a rough couple of weeks."

Kate nodded. "Aaron told me about your friend." She glanced down at my hand, still on the door. "May I come in?"

Briefly, I considered telling Kate about Lily in revenge, that Aaron had asked her out finally and she had said yes. Instead, I opened the door wider and she followed me into the kitchen. We sat at the table, diagonal from each other. "I'm sorry for your loss."

"Thanks," I mumbled. The last person I wanted to talk about Kim to was Kate.

She looked around. "Is Marina with her, uh, birth mom today?"

"She's with Zora. They're at the mall."

"Why didn't you go?"

"Marina's trying to surprise me for my birthday," I said. "October."

Kate laughed. "I know when your birthday is. I remember."

"What is it with you and Shauna, anyway?"

"Who?"

"Marina's birth mom. Why do you hate the idea of Marina seeing her so much?"

Kate bit her lip. "I guess I think if you want Marina to see her birth mom so much, maybe you regret not knowing yours?"

Silence. "I. . . never thought about it that way."

"Oh. I just thought maybe—"

"I promise, it's not about that."

"You and Aaron always used to say that. 'It's not about you.' I just tried to do the best I could."

"I know."

"He's looking for his birth parents," she said. "Did you know that?"

"It doesn't mean he loves you less."

"I know. I am trying, Sadie. With both of you." She reached her hand forward, and I pulled mine back. Not yet. She cleared her throat. "Is there. . . anything you want to say?"

I frowned. "Like?"

"I don't know. You're always telling me I do all the talking."

I shrugged. "I guess I just never thought about it as the same. You adopted us so young and you didn't even know who my birth parents were."

"But you never. . ."

"No. You were enough parent for me to handle."

The corners of Kate's mouth twitched up. "I suppose that's fair."

I gave her a small smile. "I don't know, I guess it's also that you adopted because you couldn't have kids, like, biologically. And I could, but, you know, fell in love with someone else who didn't make sperm."

"I really do love Zora, for the record."

"Yeah."

"I worried that you and Aaron wouldn't be close because you weren't related by blood. But I was so wrong. And I guess my sister and I were blood related and. . . You know what happened."

"Mmhmm." My Aunt Robin had married a man who controlled her, who had been jealous of the relationship between her and Kate. Someone who split them, just like their own mom had. Just like Kate did to me and Aaron sometimes, even though we wouldn't let her succeed.

"I miss her," she said.

"I'm sorry."

Kate reached out again, and I let her take my hand this time. "I really am sorry about your friend, Sadie."

I blinked back tears, and Kate squeezed my hand. "Me too," I said.

***

Zora held onto my arm as we walked through the gravestones. Some of them were surrounded by family plots. Others sat alone. We kept walking until we got to a small, gray stone with just one date from the year before.

Asher Goldman-Walker.

I sat on my knees in front of the stone and placed the daisies we'd brought on it. The florist we'd gone to had tried to tell us all about which flowers represented death and life and love and all that, but in the end, we picked the daisies because they were there, and they were beautiful.

Zora kneeled beside me. "I think he would have liked them," she said.

"He wouldn't have known what to do with them. He would have been one," I said. I leaned against Zora and she put her arm around me. "Did you come here a lot?"

"Sometimes. When you were admitted. The six month anniversary. Sometimes when I worried he might be lonely."

"Did you bring Marina?"

"No. I wanted to wait for you to do that." She took my hand. "Are you okay?"

"Mmhmm." I was crying, and my heart hurt, but I really was okay. For now.

"Do you want me to go away, so you can talk to him?"

"No. Don't leave." I leaned forward and put a hand on the stone. It was warm under the sun, cool in the spots where the leaves provided their shade. "I love him."

"Me too." She squeezed my shoulder. "He would have been proud of you too. Or, he would have been once he was old enough."

I leaned up and kissed her. "I love you." We stayed that way for a while, holding each other in front of Asher's grave. At some point, long after my knees started to ache and we'd both run out of tears, we stood, wiping our sorrow from each other's faces. We linked hands and together, we walked home.

EPILOGUE:
THE LAST LETTER

Dear Marina,

When I first met you, Marina, you were two years old, and you were already my everything. A social worker brought you and Shauna to meet us at our apartment. Shauna cried, and so did we. You were wearing a dress with little rabbits on them, and from then on, you were Bunny.

Zora and I had talked about you for the longest time, before we even knew who you were. We wanted you so badly. We talked for hours long into the night about what you might look like, if you would love the beach like me or want to be a doctor like her. Shauna let us love you, and we're always be grateful to her for that.

It was hard at first, and I'm sure it's hard for any parent, but it's hard in an isolating way. No one talks about what they go through when they adopt a child, especially an older child. Your Uncle Aaron was an incredible support, and so were Kim and Terry. Zora's parents loved you right away. What made it so hard was that my own mother, Kate, planted seeds of doubt in my mind. They spread and grew as you did.

You bonded with Zora first, asked for her every time I held you and reached for her when she came. It was natural to bond with one of us first, and of course we grew close so quickly, but those few weeks where you didn't want me stuck with me for a long time. Every decision I made, I second guessed myself. Especially when I decided to have Asher, I wondered if you would feel left out. You never did. You were thrilled to be an older sister. I'm glad we can still give that to you.

We weren't sure for a while if we were ready to have another child, but we still wanted one, and we wanted you to be a big sister because you would be so amazing at it, for one, and more importantly, it would make you so happy. And just like with you, we loved Kamala from the moment we met her. She was five years old when her social worker brought her to us, and she immediately sat on my lap, holding my hand. She was ours.

Feeling Asher growing inside me when I was pregnant only made me feel closer to you. Do you remember how helpful you were? You sat with me and Zora trying to pick names for the baby. In Judaism, we name children after previous generations, but only with the first letter of their name. You came to us Marina, but you still wanted Asher to have an "A" name, after Zora's mom, Angel. We tried to explain to you that the person had to be dead, but I don't really practice anyway and Zora was only going to indulge me because why not, so we chose Asher. You tried to help us paint what would be Asher's room purple, but ended up getting more of it in your hair than on the walls. You wanted to come with us to doctor's appointments and make sure the doctor knew that the baby didn't like orange juice, since it made him kick. This was very important to you.

Losing Asher made me feel like I'd lost that connection with you too. The immediate pain of losing my son never lessened that month after, but other hurts piled on. The friends that had been so excited over his birth never came by to shoulder some of the burden of his death. I heard Zora crying softly when she disassembled the furniture in Asher's room. Perhaps worst though was the loss of you persistently by my side, making sure I drank plenty of water and avoided getting near sharp object that you were afraid would puncture my expanding stomach.

I'm working on feeling guilty now. I've been in therapy for two years and we've worked on quite a bit, actually. I felt guilty when your Aunt Kim got sick and had to fight for her life so soon after I'd tried to end mine. I felt guilty when I made people uncomfortable just by being after I'd been released from the psych hospital, like Talia, whom you may not remember. The most guilt I've ever felt though was over you and Zora. What would have happened to you both if I had succeeded? Logic tells me I was sick, but I can't help that small voice in the back of my brain that tells me how selfish I was, how much I put you both through. I'll maybe have that voice forever, but Rosa is helping me figure out not to listen to it.

Bunny, you have been the most incredible part of my life. Watching you grow and learn and figure things out has been the most amazing experience and I wouldn't change a second of it. I'm so excited to watch you teach Kamala all you know. Asher would have been so lucky to have you as his big sister, but I'm glad Kamala will get this chance.

It's still incredible to me how much capacity you have for love, how much you already care about the people in your life. When I went back to teaching, you were over the moon for me. When my agent found a publisher for my novel about a thirty-something coping with depression while her best friend deals with cancer, you screamed so loud with joy, even though you didn't really know what it meant for me. When Uncle Aaron and Aunt Lily asked you to be the flower girl at their wedding, you were so thrilled, and even more so when you found out you would be getting young cousins, though Lily isn't sure how she feels about giving birth to twins. When Uncle Terry said no to a date with that woman from his work, you sat him down and told him that he couldn't be sad forever. You had just turned eight. He went, and it was a disaster, but it was a start.

I'm still not sure if I'm a good parent. Maybe you'll be in therapy one day talking about your crazy mom. I try so hard though, because that's what you deserve. You deserve to have love, and you deserve to be happy. You deserve to be surrounded by people you love and who love you. You deserve the world, my Marina, and I can only give you what I have. I hope it's enough.

Love forever and always,
Mom

ACKNOWLEDGEMENTS

In 2009, I spent five days in a psych hospital for suicidal ideation. After, no one spoke about it. One friend knew about the real reason I'd been gone, and the rest all heard that I'd needed my "meds adjusted in a controlled setting." After that, nothing.

It was extremely isolating, being the only one I knew in my life who'd spent time in an inpatient facility, the only one I knew taking Prozac or who spent at least two afternoons a week going to doctors and therapists and psychiatrists. I apologized for having panic attacks or bailing on plans because of an appointment because I believed these were things I should be able to control. I wouldn't find out until much later, after I finally started speaking out about my own experiences, that others I knew had gone through similar traumas.

Sadie is just one person, and a fictional person at that. She does not represent everyone who has ever dealt with depression or suicidal ideation. But my hope is that readers might be able to see themselves in her and know they aren't alone. Maybe by telling her story, I can challenge the stigma around mental health just the smallest bit.

There are so many people to acknowledge regarding this book, so forgive me if I leave anyone out. First, Beatriz, Elizabeth, Leah, and Rachel, who have been supporting me in all of my endeavors for years. All of them read a few chapters of this book long before I was ready for the rest of the world to see it, and it was because of them that I kept going. Thank you to Beatriz, Michelle, and Rachel, who read the rest much more than the first few chapters when I was ready for someone else to make sure I wasn't crazy for wanting to send this off to agents and publishing houses. Thank you to Nick at Atmosphere Press for believing in this manuscript and to my editor Alex, who helped make it shine.

Thanks to everyone who's ever spoken about their own mental health journeys, especially Ariel, Em, Emily, Danni, Maria, and Molly Anne, my personal heroes. You make it easier for the rest of us just to be. Shout out to the Mayo Clinic and the American Cancer Society, both of which gave me a ton of information about leukemia and brain cancer, among other things.

To the readers who make stories like these possible to tell. Thank you for caring. Thank you for reading.

ABOUT ATMOSPHERE PRESS

Atmosphere Press is an independent, full-service publisher for excellent books in all genres and for all audiences. Learn more about what we do at atmosphere-press.com.

We encourage you to check out some of Atmosphere's latest releases, which are available at Amazon.com and via order from your local bookstore:

This Side of Babylon, a novel by James Stoia
Within the Gray, a novel by Jenna Ashlyn
Where No Man Pursueth, a novel by Micheal E. Jimerson
Here's Waldo, a novel by Nick Olson
Tales of Little Egypt, a historical novel by James Gilbert
For a Better Life, a novel by Julia Reid Galosy
The Hidden Life, a novel by Robert Castle
Big Beasts, a novel by Patrick Scott
Alvarado, a novel by John W. Horton III
Nothing to Get Nostalgic About, a novel by Eddie Brophy
GROW: A Jack and Lake Creek Book, a novel by Chris S
    McGee
Home is Not This Body, a novel by Karahn Washington
Whose Mary Kate, a novel by Jane Leclere Doyle
Stuck and Drunk in Shadyside, a novel by M. Byerly
These Things Happen, a novel by Chris Caldwell

ABOUT THE AUTHOR

Nicole Zelniker (she/her) is a writer, activist, and podcast producer at *The Nasiona*. Nicole is also the author of *Mixed*, a non-fiction book about race and mixed-race families, and *Last Dance*, a collection of short stories. Check out the rest of her work at nicolezelniker.com.